I stood there blindly while she kissed me.

She whispered, "I've been wanting to do that for a long time."

"We've only known each other a month."

"Don't argue."

When I could see her mouth, I kissed her back. And stopped. To kiss her I'd had to lean in. I could feel her warmth and solidness, and her breasts. My hands were on her shoulders, hers rested on my waist. Standing like that made me realize how often I lived in a state of tension, as though the cells in my skin vibrated and the tremors passed inward until my internal organs hummed and shivered. Under Ryan's touch, the quivering ceased.

She seemed to feel me relax and drew me out of the kitchen. We sat on the futon and held hands.

She asked, "Couldn't you tell I was attracted to you?"

"I didn't think about it."

"You think about everything."

"Today, when I was cooking, I thought I was probably attracted to you."

She was thoughtful. "So when you invited me to dinner — ?"

"I didn't know." I blurted, "I'm a virgin."

ENDLESS LOVE

LISA SHAPIRO

THE NAIAD PRESS, INC.
1998

Printed in the United States of America on acid-free paper
First Edition

Editor: Christine Cassidy
Cover designer: Bonnie Liss (Phoenix Graphics)
Typesetter: Sandi Stancil

Library of Congress Cataloging-in-Publication Data

Shapiro, Lisa, 1962 –
    Endless love / by Lisa Shapiro.
        p.   cm.
    ISBN 1-56280-213-5   (alk. paper)
    I. Title.
PS3569.H34146E53   1998
813'.54—dc21   98-13235
                                                      CIP

For Lynne,
who sees the colors.

Acknowledgments

My heartfelt thanks and gratitude go to Gina Sperry, Head Coach, Women's Cross Country/Track & Field at the University of New Hampshire, and Gary O'Neil, President, OGBE Communications, both of whom gave graciously of their time and expertise.

For sharing research notes and Italian cookies, special thanks to Mika Meadows and Gwen Gallassio. Thanks also to Martha Morrison, reader, Ann Russell and Bonnie Spencer, the seminarians, and Kate Giordano at the reference desk at the Portsmouth, New Hampshire Public Library. I am also indebted to Seymour Dussman for his loving and generous support.

Lynne D'Orsay, my partner, is an integral and essential part of my writing process. I doubt that I could reach the depths without her help. My devout thanks and love to her.

About the Author

Lisa Shapiro lives with Lynne D'Orsay and Hannah D'Orsay Gardner in their new home in Tampa, Florida. Lynne and Lisa have been together for twelve years.

Also by Lisa Shapiro

The Color of Winter
Sea to Shining Sea

PART I
To Life

Chapter 1

"Love is endless." She said those words at the very beginning. "Something like this can't go away. It won't fade or disappear. There's too much emotion. The feeling's too strong."

I propped myself up on an elbow. She reached for my breast, surrounded it with her open palm. I closed my eyes and forgot to protest. She released my breast and put her hands on my shoulders, pulling me down. But I was never one to let go of an argument.

I resisted. "Wait a minute."

She smiled. "I don't want to wait."

I lay on top. I was smaller, thinner, shorter. She didn't move, pretending that my weight was too much, that I could pin her and keep her down. I felt her abdominal muscles harden as she laughed.

"What's so funny?"

"You look so serious."

"You're talking about eternity. You can't just make a profound statement, toss it off and let it go without discussion."

"You're so academic. It's one of the things I love about you." She stroked my hips.

I inched higher, rubbing myself on her sternum. She inhaled. With a groan, I came. She caught me as I slipped forward. So easily.

"Did you mean it?" I whispered. "About endless love?"

She kept kissing me. "Yes."

Early in the fall of my junior year at college, a corkboard advertisement at the student union had brought her to my apartment. Her voice on the phone, when she called to set a time, was pleasantly deep. Holding a pot of ramen noodles, I opened the door.

"Andrea Stern? I'm Ryan Mann."

I noticed her confidence first. It was apparent in the way she held her head, as though a garland crowned her short brown hair. Freckles sprinkling her nose and cheeks might have made her look puckish, except for the seriousness in her dark blue eyes. The

4

difference in our height was the second distinction I made.

She looked down at me, taking in the quilted potholder and pan of noodles. I'd just taken the pot off the stove and a fork protruded from the squiggly mass of pasta.

I wiped my free hand on my jeans. "Hi."

"I'm not early." She shook my hand and stepped inside. At least I'd made the bed. If I didn't fold the futon, I couldn't get into the kitchen. She asked, "Weren't you expecting me?"

"Um, I wasn't sure you'd come." In the kitchen, I set the pot on the stove and took two bowls from a cupboard. "Want some ramen?"

"Sure."

She set her backpack on the floor and watched as I dished up the noodles. I chopped a scallion and tossed it in.

"Red pepper?" I held up a pouch with Chinese lettering on it and sprinkled some into my bowl.

She turned her head quickly and sneezed. "No, thanks." She reached for a paper towel and blew her nose.

My table was metal-rimmed Formica, cozy for two, squeezed against the wall between the futon and the door.

When we were seated, she asked, "How long have you been tutoring?"

I stuck my nose deeper into my bowl, slurping noodles. My glasses fogged. "You're the first."

"I guess you don't have references."

The cloth napkins on my table matched the quilted potholder. They'd belonged to my grandmother.

"You said English and history, right?" I pointed to her backpack. "Let me see your books." She unpacked half a dozen volumes. "Where's the rest?" She looked surprised and I said, "I told you on the phone, I took those classes two years ago. Comparative literature and American history, colonies to the Civil War. The reading lists haven't changed. You're four books short for lit."

"I'm already a paper behind."

We were three weeks into the fall semester. "I thought you said you were a sophomore. This is freshman lit."

"I had to take an incomplete last semester."

"I got A's in both of those classes. My GPA's three point nine-eight. Do you need any other references?"

"What happened to the other point zero-two?"

"General requirements. I got an A minus in math. It's harder to intuit the answers."

Her voice sharpened. "What does that mean?"

"I can usually tell what questions will be on the exam. For essays and papers, I almost always know what angle the teacher is looking for. Getting good grades isn't just about studying the material. You have to lay it out, present it in a way so the teacher knows — this student gets it. It's a symbiotic relationship," I explained. I'd also taken freshman biology and I was showing off. "School's not a vacuum. The professors need to know they taught you something."

"Can you teach me to do that?"

"Sure." I tried to sound confident.

I'd never put my theory into words, had never tried to describe what it was to listen to a teacher

6

and know what they wanted. But every class had a nuance, a subtle undercurrent. When I found it, tapped it, everything flowed. It was a kind of intuition that had carried me into my junior year of college with nearly flawless grades. I had no idea if it was something I could teach.

On the phone, we'd agreed on fifteen dollars an hour, two hours per session twice a week. Ryan took out her wallet and extracted several crisp twenties. They looked fresh from an automatic teller machine. She was going to pay the week's sixty dollars up front. I eyed the money, glad that I'd passed her interview.

Each year the grants and financial assistance left me with a tuition gap to fill, and I was already deeper into student loan debt than I cared to think about. I'd budgeted for rent and utilities. If the winter wasn't too cold, I'd get by. At Durham University in New Hampshire, winter was always cold.

For two years I'd filled my out-of-class hours with secretarial and library assistant jobs, a schedule that proved longer and more exhausting than any reading list. I'd also tried waitressing but made such lousy tips it wasn't worth it. The real problem was time. In another semester I had to submit packages to graduate schools, and no writing program was going to consider me without samples. *I'll get up earlier tomorrow*, or, *I'll stay up tonight and write* were prayers that boiled away like steam from a kettle. If I didn't make the time now, I never would. There would always be more money to earn, fewer hours in which to think, dream, compose.

Last semester my grandmother had died. "So,"

she used to poke me. "Andrea, when are you going to write a book?"

"Soon, Grandma."

She'd always pressed a few bills into my hand. "All the studying you do. All those brains and you forget to eat."

This year, Rosh Hashanah had come and gone without a holiday card and gift of money tucked inside. It was up to me to earn the money for my food. It was up to me to find the time to write.

I eyed the money lying on my table and felt a flash of anger. I knew that Ryan was on an athletic scholarship. The campus paper was full of her name. "Track Star, Ryan Mann" and "Mann, Olympic Hopeful" were headlines that even a klutz like me couldn't miss.

Not for the first time, I regretted choosing Durham University. For what it cost, I could have gone to one of the small literary colleges in Vermont. Durham was strong in business and sports. Or I could have stayed in Massachusetts, paid less tuition and lived closer to my mother's irrational anger. She wasn't mad at me for the usual reasons — I made good grades, excellent grades, and I'd scraped together an enviable financial aid package. After the first year, I hadn't asked her for tuition assistance. I was my father's daughter; she was my sister's mother. It wasn't my fault, or so I tried to believe, that my sister had let her down.

At the time I applied to college, Mom and I were fighting nonstop. To each other, my divorced parents were cordially icy. My father, upon learning of my application to Durham, wrote me a check on the spot. He was doing his own adolescent rebellion and supported my acting out.

"New Hampshire is cold," my grandmother had worried. "You'll freeze."

"It's all New England, Grandma. It's cold here, too."

"It's not the same," she'd warned.

Oddly, she was right. New Hampshire seemed starker, although its winters were no more white, its summers just as green as those in Massachusetts. Storms in the Berkshires blew as fiercely as those across the Presidential range. In both states, small towns were laced like beads on strings of two-lane highways, the cities between molded from the same urban components. But New Hampshire felt colder, more remote.

My anger faded. I scooped up Ryan's money and shook her hand. She needed tutoring; I needed cash. The dumb jock and the bookworm. Some match.

Chapter 2

On Mondays we reviewed her weekly assignments and discussed the reading she'd done over the weekend. At first I made suggestions for her papers; after a couple of weeks, she began to outline her own arguments. On Thursdays I edited her drafts, questioned each premise and forced her to give specific, supporting detail. Her dedication surprised me. She wasn't dumb, as I'd first supposed, and she genuinely wanted to learn. But she had no instincts when it came to studying. She hobbled herself by paying equal attention to every detail, unable to discern between crucial and lesser facts.

"How do you know it won't be on the test?" she asked when I told her to skip a section and move on.

I sighed. "Stop worrying about single events and start thinking in terms of patterns."

"Explain that." She got demanding when she was frustrated.

"You're studying out of context." I pushed a stack of books toward her. "This isn't a random reading list. The professor wants to tie it all together. You need to get the overview, understand the relationships and give examples."

"I have to write papers on each book. Not everything is compare and contrast, you know."

"You'll get a better grade," I said quietly, "if you build one paper on another. Compare anyway. Teachers love that."

She crossed her arms. "Is this a game to you or what?"

"I really enjoy studying. And yes, in a way it is a game. I'm good at it."

She glowered but finally uncrossed her arms, picked up a pencil. "It's not enough to get good grades. I need to . . . I want to . . . understand. I want other people to understand what I'm trying to say."

I said gently, "Seeing the patterns and building on themes are the best ways to do that. Everything else is format." I gave her an encouraging smile. "Give it to them the way they want it. You can learn a lot and never get good grades, but then what's the point of paying tuition?"

She laughed. "It's easier to study here."

"It must get pretty noisy in the dorms."

"It's not the noise. I have trouble in the library, too. I start questioning everything and then I go back, change my outline, doubt my answers. You're so organized. It helps me stay on track."

"Study here." The words were out of my mouth before I could stop them. I read the hesitation on her face. Even scholarship students had budget constraints. But I hadn't meant it like that. "You don't have to pay," I said quickly. "It's not tutoring, just study time. Everyone has study partners. You can be mine."

"You don't need a partner. You get the right answers by yourself."

"I study better when you're here," I admitted.

Since I'd started tutoring Ryan, I was more efficient. I outlined her course strategies, then mine. I got to the same place in the long run, but working with her, I got there faster.

There was another reason, too, that niggled. I liked the company. I'd begun my college career on a note of defiance and then turned into a recluse. I sat alone in class, lived alone and studied by myself in my apartment. I knew people, in the way that seeing the same faces every day breeds familiarity without intimacy. And I knew that, once my schooling was complete, I wouldn't stay in New Hampshire. A feeling of impermanence had combined with my natural shyness to turn me into a hermit.

I imagined my grandmother's scolding. *"Andrea, all day you sit by yourself. Get out. Make friends. How do you expect to meet someone?"*

Ryan began to study at my place and I soon learned the rigors of her schedule.

Every morning she went running.

"How far do you go?" I asked.

"Three and a half or four miles. It's for conditioning. I'm not a distance runner."

"How long does it take?"

"About twenty-five minutes. Do you like to run?"

"I don't think so." I said more definitely, "No."

When I was twelve, before my parents got divorced, my father had taken the family on a camping trip. There are dozens of places to camp in Massachusetts, but he packed us on a plane to California, rented a car and drove to Yosemite. Dad was a fan of grandeur. I read two books during the five-hour plane trip and passed the car ride in an agony of motion sickness. Gorgeous, dangerous ravines dropped away from the mountain highway. The guardrail would help little if my father took the plunge, rental car and family combined, over the edge.

On the valley floor, our cabin came equipped with running water and electricity.

"This is the life," Dad assured us.

For years afterward, I had a recurring nightmare that my father really had driven himself over a cliff. In my imagination, the remainder of the family — Mom, sister Julia, myself — were safely out of harm's way. I was never clear if Dad's demise was accidental, or if a higher power, having noticed our sins, had demanded recompense. In my journal, I wrote a shockingly vivid account of screeching, dented metal. I envisioned rocks like leaded boxing gloves

13

pummeling his car until it was crushed, deflated, my father defeated.

One night I awakened with fear clamping my jaw, cracking my neck — the fear that somehow the nightmare had come to pass, that my father, out late and driving home, had crashed and died. And I would have made it happen. Not for wanting it — I didn't want my father to die — but for dreaming it. I imagined God, the owner of those rocky fists, picking chipped car paint from between his craggy knuckles.

God looked at my father's limp bones, shattered body, and said, "Nice idea, Andrea. That worked like a charm."

One year when the nightmares were particularly bad, I gave up reading fiction. It didn't help, though. Mom and Dad got divorced, and unless I saw him on the weekend or called him in the evening, I had no way of knowing if he'd made it home in one piece. Sometimes I'd used the pay phone at school and called him at the office, just to do a spot check that he was still okay.

Ryan's training was relentless. Pre-season began in the fall, and the winter meets were held at the field house. In spring, the track and field events moved outside. She practiced every afternoon. Four days a week, her workouts included a session at the weight room. She was building power, she explained, for the sprints and throws. She returned to her dorm for dinner and then carried her books to my apartment, exuding the kind of confidence that belongs to the superbly physically fit.

* * * * *

On that last excessive vacation, my family had traveled too far, camped with too many accessories and climbed impossibly high, steep trails. Some children dream that they can fly. I used to dream that I could run, sprint, hit a tennis ball or climb a fence. For me, effortless physical activity was unattainable freedom.

"I'll rest here," I said again and again.

"I hope you brought a book," Dad teased.

Mom said shrilly, "Samuel Stern, you will not leave your daughter behind on this trail."

Julia, three years older than me, was in front, tan legs flexed as though the mountain were nothing more than a vertical tennis court. I sat on a rock and attempted an argument.

"Dad, you have smart children and you take pride in our individuality." He often made that statement.

Mom is beautiful, I wanted to add, but Julia had crept into my room one night while Mom and Dad were fighting. "Dad's having an affair," she'd whispered.

"If you have a point, Andrea, we're waiting."

Dad loved playing judge to my lawyer. It was a parlor game, meant to be played at bedtime with a brandy for him, hot chocolate for me. The vicious mountainside was no place to take on my father or his guilt.

"I just want to remind you that only one of your daughters is an athlete. You can't turn a bookworm into a hiker overnight." I pictured myself with a segmented body, no arms or legs, just a wiggling, worm-like tail attached to my head. Even as a worm

15

I wore glasses. The weight of my backpack squashed me flat.

Dad laughed, dragged me to my feet and propelled me forward. He called out the steps in sing-song fashion. "One, two, three, four." He sang, "This is how you pass the test. Never let your tushie rest." Dad always won our arguments.

Finally, we reached a plateau. Across the valley, twin waterfalls dripped. They looked like the long ribbons tied in my sister's hair, twisting away from her as she ran. The wispy, distant streams were so lovely that I forgot our family misery. I forgot my mother's thin anger. I forgot to resent Julia's greater strength. I believed that Dad had bought us a gift, as though he'd gone to the mall, come home and set up the waterfalls in our living room. Julia stood triumphantly. She was used to attaining peaks.

A voice in my head said, *Stern family discovers natural beauty. In spite of themselves.*

I squinted. Above the twin falls there was a third sparkling stream, a trickle not yet joined to the rest.

Fingers dug into my arm. "Andrea, get away from the edge!" Mom sounded hysterical.

She dragged me back. Later, when they began to fight, I imagined both of my parents going over the cliff.

Chapter 3

Ryan hefted her backpack onto my table and began to unload her books.

"Leave them here," I suggested. "You only study here." I suspected her of lugging them around to prove her strength.

She shook her head. "I need to feel like I have a separate intellect." Her insight surprised me. She'd also taken up teasing me, which I figured was her way of leveling the turf. More than once, she'd said, "You're cute when you concentrate."

I got used to it and ignored it. She had to be

teasing. Jocks like Ryan had nothing to do with scrawny, academic types like me. They looked over my head, brushed past my unmuscular shoulders. I decided it was her way of telling me that she was comfortable with our study arrangement.

I also learned that she was devoted to her family. She reserved Sundays for them and they all went to church.

One evening she asked, "Do you practice Judaism?"

"Not really." I fingered the candlesticks I kept on the table.

"Those are beautiful."

"They were my grandmother's."

"Do you light the Sabbath candles?"

"You didn't tell me you were studying comparative religion."

"Sorry."

I hadn't meant to snap. "My grandmother died last March. I, um, don't have any candles. Let's study, okay?"

Religion was the one subject I avoided. I'd never learned Hebrew, had never been Bat Mitzvahed. I'd started the program and then dropped out, and my lack of religious education had been a disappointment to my grandmother. I remembered her arguing with Dad, her son, but he was satisfied with my secular studies. It wasn't just ignorance of the language, however. I lacked faith. It wasn't a test where I could intuit the answers. Faith was a way of knowing I didn't understand.

Ryan looked up from her notebook. "What's the matter?"

"Do you want to come over tomorrow? We can,

um, do an extra study session. I'll make dinner." I tried to sound casual but inwardly I cringed. Tomorrow was Friday.

Ryan said, "Six o'clock?"

The next evening while I cooked, I thought about her and my grandmother. I'd used Ryan's tutorial money to buy a roasting chicken, and I boiled rice flavored with the pan drippings. Last year at Hanukkah, I'd cooked a chicken for my grandmother, removing the skin to cut down on fat.

She'd laughed at me. "You think you're going to save my life by drying out the meat and making it taste bad? Is that any way to treat an old lady?"

"It's better for you this way, Grandma."

"So, at your age you suddenly know what's best? Tell me, how did you get to be such a know-it-all?" She kept up her discourse throughout the meal. "A little schmaltz never killed a Jew. There's plenty of Arabs trying to kill us, but not with the skin of a roasting chicken. Andrea, if you want to live a healthy life, keep your politics out of the kitchen. Cooking is for love. If you really love someone, it's okay to make them a little fat." She'd tapped my hand with a forceful finger. "You hear?"

This time I left the skin on. Ryan was strong enough to take it. I was thin enough. And Grandma was right — it tasted better. I cut up broccoli and put it in a steamer pan. Chicken fat was one thing; vitamins were another matter. I prowled through my spice cabinet and chose savory for the chicken, salt and pepper for the broccoli.

When the rice was simmering and the chicken skin browning, I settled onto my futon and picked up a book. But my mind began to wander. I pictured

Ryan in high-waisted trousers and a soft turtleneck sweater. I wondered where the unbidden image was coming from. She always showed up at my door in jeans and an oversized sweatshirt. If she was such an athlete, why didn't she show off her muscles? Maybe she was shy. Maybe she was out of touch with an abusive childhood, and the whole family and church thing was a cover she hadn't broken through. Perhaps, after dinner, I could engage her in a conversation about body image.

In my fantasy, Ryan, in her elegant clothes, was standing beside the table. I set the perfect roast in front of her, handed her a carving knife and said, *"Darling, would you do the honors?"*

The kitchen timer dinged. I said, "Shit," and hopped off the futon. Ryan wasn't due for half an hour. I turned down the oven temperature and muttered, "Bad planning, Stern." I'd started early because I was nervous. Now the food would be overcooked. Was I destined, always, to feed my loved ones dry chicken? "Get over yourself," I warned. But on my way back to the futon, I pulled my copy of *Our Bodies, Ourselves* off the bookshelf.

In my sophomore-year women's studies class, I'd started calling myself a lesbian. The assistant professor had written encouraging comments in my class journal and attached a supplemental reading list to my final paper. As usual, I'd earned an A. Academically, I was as out as they come, but it was an intellectual exercise. I'd only ever made love to my own hand and I still felt guilty about it. I tossed the book on the floor and closed my eyes. I imagined Ryan, dressed for dinner, carving my roast.

The knife bit into the meat and her eyes met mine. *"I'm sorry, Andrea, this won't work. Your chicken is dry as a bone."*

"Wait," I pleaded. *"Please, taste it. It's well-seasoned."*

At sundown on Friday night, my grandmother had covered her eyes to say the blessing. Julia and I, left to stay the weekend, memorized the Hebrew, mimicked the words. Grandma poured sweet wine into tall goblets. Candlelight sparkled through the glass.

At my parents' house, stretching the length of the front hall, lay an Oriental rug, a narrow strip of carpet patterned in purple, red and blue. At Grandma's, I sipped wine and pretended that someone had drawn the colors from the rug and strained them into my glass. The Sabbath wine was a link between my father's home and my grandmother's love.

She watched me take tiny sips. "That's too strong for you."

She'd opened a pop-top and poured Seven-Up into my Manischewitz. Friday night dinner at Grandma's was the first time I ever got drunk.

In my kitchen, I set the chicken on top of the stove. I wondered if Ryan would like it. I wondered if she was a lesbian or just a handsome jock. A Christian jock. Maybe I should have made ham.

I'd never tasted ham. My family had never bothered to keep a kosher household but there was a line we respected, drawn across the graves of my ancestors — milk and honey on one side, ham on the other.

In elementary school, I'd spent Saturday night at a friend's house and gone with her family to the Sunday morning church service.

"I gave up ice cream for Lent," she whispered. "I miss it so much." In the church foyer, she showed me the sign-up for the Easter potluck. "We eat ham and jelly beans."

I pictured a pink ham studded with green jelly beans that popped in the baking heat, oozing sugary glaze.

In the early days before the divorce, Mom had cooked lavishly for dinner parties. Our dining room held a glossy, richly-grained drop-leaf table. Black stripes swirled zebra-like through the golden wood. When the leaves were down, I hid under it. Boxed in and safely hidden, I pretended I was in a jungle. The colors in the wood reminded me of pancakes and crisp bacon, a Sunday morning meal when we weren't at Grandma's.

I don't know how it came to pass that, as Jews, we purchased one part of the pig and shunned the other; we ate bacon but ham never entered the house. If menus could make people crazy, then it was no wonder that, by the age of sixteen, my sister was a full-blown schizophrenic.

I answered a knock at my door and found Ryan, dressed for dinner in jeans and a blue heather pullover. A button-down collar circled her throat. Her brown hair looked freshly washed and blown-dry. Her cheeks were rosy and her freckles stood out. The blue sweater deepened the blue of her eyes.

She handed me a paper bag. "I got a bottle of red wine. Is that okay?"

The gesture delighted me. "Can you? Don't you have a meet tomorrow?" Alcohol was taboo before competitions.

She smiled shyly. "It's traditional, isn't it? I mean, for Friday night and everything."

I felt something else in the bag. "You brought candles," I exclaimed.

Her smile broadened. "It smells great in here. What's for dinner?"

"Roast chicken."

"That's my favorite."

"Really?"

"Sure. Why not?" She dumped her backpack in the corner. "I brought my books. Just in case we get around to studying." She was smiling a lot. "Do you want me to open the wine?"

I remembered that I didn't have a corkscrew. Living on my own, I ignored Friday night. I wasn't religious, so there was no reason to light candles or pour wine. I held up the bottle and examined the label before admitting the problem.

Ryan said, "I can borrow one." She headed for the door.

I said lamely, "Wait. I'm not on borrowing terms with anyone."

"A couple of girls from the team live downstairs. I'll be right back." It embarrassed me that she knew my neighbors better than I did. With Ryan around, my realm of isolation was shrinking. I stuck the tapers in my grandmother's candlesticks. Ryan returned just in time to take the matches from my shaking hand. "Let me." She tore out a match and closed the cover before striking it. Meticulous. It was one of the reasons she had trouble with her papers. She took too long over the small points. But then there was candlelight, a flickering glow. She prompted, "How about some music?"

"I just have tapes." I was embarrassed again, this time by my poverty.

She knelt to inspect my collection and pressed the play button on my beaten-up equipment. She'd picked one of my favorite folk tapes. The candlelight was stuck in her hair, trapped in the corners of her mouth. I'd forgotten the feeling of candles, the peace of them, like waking up when the sun is still orange and easy to look at, or when the shadows at sunset are long but it isn't time yet to turn on the lights.

Ryan caught me watching her. Unexpectedly, she asked, "Do you like me?"

I was taken aback. "I like you." After a moment I admitted, "You make me nervous."

"Oh." She looked uncertain. "Do you want to do this another time?"

"No." I spoke quickly, then cast around for a reason to make her stay. "Midterms are in a week. We should put in more study time." I sidled toward the kitchen. "I'll get dinner."

She stood in the kitchen doorway, her weight-lifting-enhanced body blocking my exit. When I struggled to transfer the chicken to a serving platter, she leaped forward to help. I got the rice into a bowl and remembered that I hadn't cooked the veggies.

I lit a burner and mumbled, "Just take a sec."

"What else can I do?"

My grandmother's Passover plates were in the highest cupboard. They were cobalt blue glass, long-since desecrated in my non-kosher kitchen. By far, they were the nicest dishes I owned. Ryan was tall enough to reach them without standing on a chair. While I waited for the vegetables, I watched her set the table.

"Andrea? How come I make you nervous?"

"I better check the broccoli."

I turned off the flame and lifted the lid. A rush of steam fogged my glasses. I jumped when I felt her hand on my back. The lid clattered. Through my fogged glasses her large form was a blur. Had I been able to see clearly, I might have moved back. As it was, I stood there blindly while she kissed me.

She whispered, "I've been wanting to do that for a long time."

"We've only known each other a month."

"Don't argue."

When I could see her mouth, I kissed her back. And stopped. To kiss her I'd had to lean in. I could feel her warmth and solidness, and her breasts. My hands were on her shoulders, hers rested on my waist. Standing like that made me realize how often I lived in a state of tension, as though the cells in my skin vibrated and the tremors passed inward until my internal organs hummed and shivered. Under Ryan's touch, the quivering ceased.

She seemed to feel me relax and drew me out of the kitchen. We sat on the futon and held hands.

She asked, "Couldn't you tell I was attracted to you?"

"I didn't think about it."

"You think about everything."

"Today, when I was cooking, I thought I was probably attracted to you."

She was thoughtful. "So when you invited me to dinner — ?"

"I didn't know." I blurted, "I'm a virgin."

She laughed. I tried to pull away but she kept ahold of my hand. "That explains it. I like you, but I couldn't tell if you were getting the signals. I thought maybe you didn't know about yourself."

"Why'd you kiss me?"

"Because telling you how cute you are wasn't working."

"I know I'm a lesbian. I've just never made love."

"Do you want to?"

I wet my lips. "Yeah."

Physical contact terrified me. Long ago, I'd chosen mind over matter, intellectual rather than physical pursuits. I'd taught myself to read during my sister's tennis lessons. Before she got sick, Julia did sports. I read books. The choice had lent a pattern to my life. I was like a puzzle piece with odd edges sticking out, weird curves that turned inward. The misfit. But with my nose in a book, society's roving eye barely hesitated, passed on. *Ah, a reader.* Into the academic pile I went. Better to be bookish than weird. And people, especially people like Ryan, left me alone.

"Down the line. Make your approach shot down the line. Get up to the net."

Deposited on a bench with a book and a cream soda, I listened to Mom shout instructions at my sister. Around her neck, Julia wore a delicate gold chain. *Chi,* the Hebrew word for life, clung to her sweaty chest.

26

"Move up," Mom yelled. "Get on top of it."

Hunched at the baseline, Julia waited for Mom's whipping serve. Normally she hung back after the serve, gave herself plenty of room. Mom was teaching her to rush the net on the service return — a gutsy shot. Julia lifted one foot, then the other, swayed slightly. Right before Mom hit the ball, Julia gave a little hop. When the serve came she was perfectly poised, balanced evenly on the balls of her feet. As the ball tore over the net she was already moving in on it, bearing down. She caught it on the rise and slammed a forehand down the line. A very gutsy shot. She rushed the net as Mom dug into her backhand, sent up a lob. Julia danced back and hit an overhead smash. Mom had no hope of reaching it.

Panting hard, she called, "Good. Again."

Julia rushed the net on return of serve from the deuce and advantage sides of the court. She hit the approach shot off her forehand, then the backhand. When the drill was over, they toweled off and played two sets. I sat cross-legged while I read, trying not to get splinters from the chipped wood bench. Their cries of effort became background noise. The afternoon sun heated my back and my shoulders cast a shadow over the pages.

I needed the books less at home. Dad filled the house with his opinions. When he didn't have colleagues to argue with, he put me in their place. We fought mock battles over dinner or Sunday brunch.

"Make your point," he instructed.

Mom kept quiet until she got on the tennis court. Then it was her turn to win. Much later it occurred to me that if my parents had conversed with each

27

other instead of their children, they might have saved their marriage. Julia and I had taken up tennis racquet and dictionary, respectively, each apprenticed to a parent. Competing as sisters, we never learned to share.

Ryan was cuddling me. Gradually, the comfortable pressure tightened. All of a sudden, I panicked and pushed her away. She was so physical, so strong. I'd never be able to stand up to her. My fear was instinctive and I regretted it immediately.

She looked hurt. "Hey."

I stumbled to the kitchen, grabbed a paper towel and swiped my eyes. I was crying.

She got up. "I guess I'd better leave."

"Don't go." I rushed to stop her. "I'm sorry I got scared."

"You acted like I was gonna attack you."

"I'm new at this. I don't know what I'm supposed to do."

She smiled a little. "I can see that." She moved into the kitchen, carried the cold chicken to the table, sliced and served. I inched closer. She asked, "Want me to pour the wine?"

"Okay."

She set a glass by my plate and reached for her backpack. I panicked again, afraid she would leave, but she pulled out a handful of papers.

"Will you take a look? It's my outline and introduction for my comparative lit midterm."

While she ate, I scanned the outline and read the penciled paragraphs through twice. "You have too many major points."

"I think they're all important."

It was one of the big differences between us. I was always looking for a pattern, a connection. She liked to take one thing at a time, go over it from every angle.

"If you're going to use all this, you need a theme to tie it together."

"I want to take each point in sequence."

"That might work." I handed back the papers.

"Is that all you're going to say?"

The more I thought about it, the more I liked her logic. "It's a good idea. Write about each one and draw separate conclusions. Show how they're balanced but distinct." When I could see the outline from her point of view, I began to get excited. "Just don't forget to give examples," I warned.

She was smiling. "You're confident when you're doing schoolwork. I'm pretty confident about everything else. We're not so different."

Her glass was empty so I poured more wine. *"L'Chaim."* I raised my wineglass.

"What does that mean?"

"It's a toast. It means, 'to life.' "

She raised her glass. "To life and to love." My shaking hand sent my glass crashing into hers and wine spilled on her jeans. I grabbed a napkin. She nabbed my hand. "You're flunking seduction one-oh-one."

I nodded miserably. "I know."

I cleared the dishes, wrapped the leftovers and hid in the kitchen until the sink was full of suds, the pans soaking. I glanced into the other room. Ryan was sitting calmly on the futon. She patted the seat beside her.

I sat down and crossed my arms. "I hate this. I hate being so scared." I was afraid I might start crying again.

"You're stubborn. Any other girl would've kicked me out a long time ago."

One of her hands rested between us. We weren't touching.

I want you to touch me. "I want —" My teeth began to chatter.

"I'm sorry," she whispered. "I made a pass too soon. Andrea? I like you. I just want you to know that."

I scooted a little closer. "Why?"

She sighed. "This has got to be the only come-on in history where I have to write an essay." She drew a leg up, clasped her knee. "You're shy, like a mouse. You won't talk about anything but books. I assume you go to class, but I've never seen you outside of this apartment." She averted her gaze. "You remind me of the way I feel when I compete. The thing I like about track and field is that I'm really competing against myself, trying to beat my own time, set a new personal best. Sometimes, right before a meet, some athletes start to generate heat. They get . . . hot. I can sense it." She glanced at me. "You have it. When you study, you get hot. That's something else we have in common."

I stared at her. I no longer felt like crying. "You're an analogist."

"What?"

"You explain one thing by showing how it resembles another. If you do that in a paper, there isn't a teacher on campus who won't give you an A."

"You mean like Shakespeare and the shot put? That'll go over well."

"Not the shot put. The rest of life. Can't you talk about anything but sports?"

"Can't you talk about anything but books?"

"My sister used to play tennis." Instantly, I was nervous again.

Ryan picked up my hand. "Tell me about her."

"She was the athletic one. My parents divided up the family. Mom took Julia, Dad got me. Sort of like choosing up sides for softball. I bet you always got picked first."

"I was team captain. I got to choose."

"People like you made my life hell."

"Not me."

"Oh, come on. The jocks never picked the wimps. I got left until you had no choice."

"Not me," she repeated.

"You pick a team to win. That's what I would do."

"So, if you were going to have a debate, you'd leave me off your team?"

I swallowed. "Yeah. I mean, I would have. Maybe not now."

"I guess my parents drummed it into me that I had to let everyone take a turn. Because I'm bigger. My kid sister's only ten. When I'm home, I do my warm-up laps with her. She's already a good athlete."

"What's her name?"

"Brittany."

I said, "Julia had her first psychotic break when she was sixteen."

"Does she still play tennis?"

"She was in and out of psych hospitals. The year I started college, three summers ago, she went into a residential program. They keep coming up with new medications. She hasn't done a suicide attempt since she's been living in the program."

"Hey, Julia. I brought you a book." It had been the only gift I could think to bring. I set it on the bed. It was June, Julia's first weekend in the program. I stared around at the blank walls of her bedroom.

"Isn't that nice," Mom said with forced cheerfulness. Dad wasn't there. They were long since divorced and Mom had finally put our mausoleum of a home on the market. Live-in psychiatric care was expensive. "Andrea, say goodbye and wait outside."

Impulsively, I kissed Julia's cheek. Mom looked stricken. I wanted to say, *Relax. Dad's gone and Julia's locked up. No one can steal your daughter.* I said, " 'Bye, sis."

"Andrea?"

"Yeah?"

"I forgot how to read. Will you teach me?" She giggled. "I'll teach you how to hit a killer serve."

"Didn't Mom tell you? I got accepted to college in New Hampshire. No one reads up there. The whole state's illiterate." We were both grinning.

"Andrea," Mom ordered. "Say goodbye."

It was a little easier after that, with Julia and me both out of the house. She got treatment and I was getting an education. Secretly, we'd agreed to get along. Mom had graduated law school. She'd decided to keep fighting with Dad.

Ryan's arm was around me. Vaguely, I remembered snuggling closer. My tears were dripping. She got up, went to my tiny bathroom and returned with a roll of toilet tissue.

I blew my nose and snuggled back down. Her arm tightened. We stayed like that for a while, until I was sure I was done crying. I'd taken my glasses off, but I didn't need them when I lifted my head. Our noses were practically touching.

She whispered, "I always used to pick someone like you to be on my team."

"To be nice? Like running slow with your sister?"

"I thought if I let the brainy girls onto the playground, they might give me a peek at their notes."

"Didn't anyone ever share their homework with you?"

"Just you, Andrea. I'm gonna kiss you now, okay?"

I closed my eyes and stopped breathing. The world stopped moving, the moon stopped sending light, gravity released its grip on me and I floated. A tiny voice in my mind said, *This is what it's like to be good at sports.*

When her arms loosened, gravity came crashing back but I didn't wrench away. There was a tiny space between our bodies, a small pocket of air separating our breasts. I summoned my strength and hurled myself through it.

She laughed as I bumped up against her. "Do you want to try that again?" She took my arms from around her neck and pulled me to my feet.

"What?" I groped for my glasses. She tugged the futon open. "Oh." I went to the closet for the comforter and pillow. I only owned one pillow.

Ryan smiled shyly and retreated to the bathroom. When she came back, she took off her shoes and lay down on top of the covers, fully clothed.

"I'll brush my teeth," I mumbled.

I tiptoed back to find the lights out, the candles still burning. It took a long time to get our clothes off. I kept stopping, listening to her breathe, listening to her heart. She stroked me through my clothes, then the skin on my back, finally the flesh of my hips. Under the covers, my hands copied hers.

The comforter was one of the first things my grandmother had paid for when I moved to college.

"Stay warm," she'd cautioned. "Study hard."

I was aware of the Sabbath candles burning, my legs entwined with Ryan's. But what I was doing had nothing to do with family, or food or shelter. This was the thing I'd found on my own, for myself.

Ryan moaned softly when I touched her breasts, reminding me that I wasn't alone, that this wasn't something I knew how to do.

"I want to make love to you," she whispered.

I said, "Touch me."

She held back. "I don't want to hurt you."

She was afraid for me. She knew her strength but she didn't know mine. She was afraid for what I could bear.

"I can take it." I wasn't worried about keeping up. If she was afraid, I would have courage. If she hesitated, I'd take her first. This was the physical thing I could do. "I'm glad you're a girl." It was the simplest thing I could think to say.

She laughed and gathered me into her. I put my hands on her chest, not to push her away but to draw her in, to draw myself inside. As she loved me, I touched her.

Through my closed eyes, I saw my hands move through the wall of her chest. The candles disappeared. All the light was from Ryan, generated by her. Inside, I could see her heart but I didn't touch it. I curled my fists like two hard plums and reached under her breastbone. There was a space there, beneath her heart, between her lungs. That's where I held my hands.

I opened my eyes. Her hips were rocking and mine responded. She shoved a hand beneath my head and one under my bottom. Our mouths were sealed together, fused.

My eyes closed. Gradually, my hands unclenched. They were within her, each palm cupped under a pumping lung.

Ryan was moving rhythmically.

Steadily, I moved through her flesh until I was up to my elbows inside her. I felt the powerful suction, damp rush of air in her bellowing lungs. Finally, I cupped her heart.

She surged on me, cried out as her whole body clenched. I felt her contractions and lost my grip. My arms slipped out leaving no hole, no opening, no wound. Her skin sealed over, airtight.

"You feel good in me," she murmured.

Dimly, I was aware that my hands were between her legs, my fingers wet. How had I known to go into her? She moved down, opened her mouth over me. When it was over, I was crying again. I grasped her shoulders, brought her up, pressed my lips to her chest. Beneath the skin, I felt her thumping heart. *I saw it.* I whispered, "I touched it."

"Hmmm?"

I said, "Don't let this end."

She said, "Love is endless."

Chapter 4

It became one of our arguments.

"Did you mean it?" I asked one evening.

Ryan was hunched over a text. "How can you start a conversation like that, in the middle of a thought?"

In my mind our discussions were ongoing. In her absence I argued both sides by myself. "Endless love," I reminded her. "Did you mean it?"

"Oh, that." Her eyes were intimate. "You're blushing. You're still shy about sex."

I bustled to the kitchen and poured a glass of

water. Ryan's chair creaked. I felt her standing behind me.

"Don't tease," I sputtered.

We'd been to bed twice — the first time, before midterms, and once after. Ryan had squeaked a B plus out of her literature essay.

"You inspired me," she'd said, and toppled me onto the futon.

She'd waited while I stripped out of my sweater and shirt. After that she didn't hesitate. She held me down and kissed me. I held her neck with one hand; with my other, I guided her fingers, crying into her collarbone when she went inside. She didn't stop until I shuddered and cried her name. When I could wriggle out, she let me push her down, then drew her legs up while I knelt. I saw her face, the streaks of tears.

"Please." She mouthed the word.

In my chest something snapped, like the strap of a backpack giving way. An image of waterfalls came into my mind, the twin falls I'd witnessed as a child. As I lay down I felt the flow begin in my belly, then her moisture under my tongue. As I sucked her in, one stream connected to another. I hadn't known, hadn't believed myself capable of such emotion. But it had been there, pouring through me.

In the kitchen she looked at me quizzically. "How can you make love to me, put your face between my legs and make me feel so good, and still be shy?"

"I'll get over it." I clutched for conversation. "About that endless love thing —"

She moved to the futon. "Do you believe in God?" I might have thought she was teasing again, but her face was serious.

"I'm agnostic." I'd been using the word since I was nine. Dad was an atheist and it delighted me to have found some philosophical difference between us. I was used to arguing that God was unknown, unknowable, even to the fact of its existence.

"You're skeptical," Ryan said. She clasped one knee with both hands, looking for all the world like a professor about to enlighten a student. I sat on the edge of the futon, uncertain where this role shift was going. She said, "I have faith in God and in our love. That doesn't mean I'm not afraid of losing you."

Her words stunned me. The fear she spoke of was uppermost in my mind, hard as I tried to push it back, tamp it down. Before Ryan, I'd been afraid of love as a timid vacationer is afraid of an unknown subway system. Having found my way into the relationship, the fear of losing her staggered me. I was afraid I'd wake up and find her gone, or watch her walk away, only to discover that she wouldn't be back.

The fear of loss was worse than anything I'd ever known. It was worse than being shy, worse even than the dread I used to feel listening to my parents fight. It had horned its way into my consciousness like a shuffling beast, a rank animal with sour breath and saliva like smoking acid.

For the love of God, I thought, calling unwittingly on her belief system. Ryan, with her strength and self-confidence, had walked right up to the monster and tapped its shoulder.

"Andrea? Are you okay?"

For a dizzying moment I wasn't in my body. I'd drawn my feet up; my hands were pressed reflexively to my chest. Ryan was next to me, bending close.

And seated on the other side, like a great dog beside his master, was the drooling, shaggy beast that her statement had unleashed. There was no way to force that kind of fear back inside. It was too massive, too big to shove back through the bottleneck between conscious and unconscious thought.

As I watched from my disembodied state, wet lips parted over serrated fangs. But there was something comical about him, like a cartoon gargoyle made to look fuzzy and cute. I had an insane urge to pat his head. We locked eyes in a childish game of chicken — me afraid to blink, him not having to. Just when I couldn't bear it any longer, his grin widened and he winked.

Rough laughter scratched my mind. *"Hah, hah. I'll win if I want to."*

I shuddered hard and was jerked back in. I felt Ryan's hand on my arm but my eyes were squeezed shut. Slowly, I opened them, peered around. The fuzzy demon was gone.

Ryan asked, "What's the matter?"

I was grateful for her touch. Without it, I feared I'd go floating off toward Hades again. I cleared my throat. "I think I had an out-of-body experience."

"Knock it off," she said briskly. "When I said I believe in God, I wasn't joking. My religion's important to me."

I rubbed my arms. My teeth were starting to chatter. I needed to move, get my circulation going. But I had the irrational, post-nightmare sense that if I stepped down my feet would be gone, snapped off by ferocious jaws.

"Call it a waking nightmare," I said. "Whatever. I just had one."

I wondered if Julia's illness had infected me. What if Mom had found a way to exorcise the schizophrenia? Set loose, it was coming after me. But I knew that what I'd just experienced didn't belong to my sister's psyche. The living, breathing, drooling fear was mine, and I didn't see how I could live with it.

Ryan said, "You're freezing," and pulled me closer.

I needed something to stuff between myself and the terror. I whispered, "Tell me about your religion. What makes you believe?"

She tucked my head under her chin. I loved it when she did that. I could feel her words when she spoke, her breath like a breeze in my hair. I closed my eyes and listened like a child to a story of make-believe. I thought the whole Jesus thing was probably a fairy tale, but as an admittedly skeptical Jew who suffered hallucinations, I didn't think I was in a position to judge. I rested my ear on her chest, listening to her heart, listening to her story.

"My great-grandparents were Catholic, from Ireland. My grandparents started going to the Episcopal church so their children would have a better chance to fit in with American culture."

"So now you're Protestant?"

"A long time ago there was just Christianity, and before Saint Patrick came to Ireland, the Celtic tradition."

"Pagan?"

"Spiritual. They felt God's presence in everything — rocks, sun, the earth, the ocean. Life was based in nature but connected to God." She pulled the necklace from under her shirt. I'd been aware of it during our lovemaking, had tangled my fingers in it but been too distracted for a closer look. Now I examined the silver pendant — the cross within a circle. "The cross stands for Christianity," she said. "The Celtic ring is a mystical symbol. Some people call it the circle of creation. It reminds me that we're all connected — in life, death and resurrection."

I held Ryan's cross, but in my mind I was looking at Julia's necklace, the delicate gold *Chi*, symbol of life. "I don't know if I believe in resurrection." But I was remembering the demon at my elbow.

Angels, devils, monsters, I chanted silently, reminding myself of a schoolyard game — rock, paper, scissors. Angels would cover the devils like paper over rock. Devils could cut the angels like scissors cut paper. And the monster would crush them both. Julia and I had played the game again and again, hands behind our backs, high voices chanting, "One, two, three!"

Ryan smoothed my hair. "I've always loved going to church. I love the music, the incense, all of it. I remember when my youth group did a prayer vigil. We stayed overnight in the chapel and went to midnight mass. It was the most beautiful, magical thing." Her cheek rested on my head. "For as long as I can remember, I've wanted to be a priest."

I was aware of being lifted, then Ryan laid me on the bed. She'd unfolded the futon. I heard water running; she was doing our dinner dishes, probably. Then she would tidy her papers and books. She was like that. Fastidious. I was sleepily aware when she lay down beside me. My back was to her and her arm came around me. I reached for her, found the hard muscle of her leg. I wanted to rouse myself, continue our conversation and then make love, but I was in the slumberous state that follows exhaustion. Terror had drained me. Ryan stroked me, her touch meant to soothe, not arouse. Feeling her strength, I fell asleep.

When I awoke in the morning, she was gone and her books with her. It made me crazy that she never left so much as a notebook in my apartment. She was generous, though, and usually showed up at my door with a bag of groceries. In the kitchen, we squabbled.

"Go easy on the garlic," she'd say. I shooed her away. I topped our salads with feta cheese and Greek olives. "Salty," she complained.

I bought a book on low-fat cooking. All that physique of hers needed good care. Practically every recipe called for skinless, broiled breast of chicken.

"Don't skin my breasts," I muttered as I furiously chopped garlic. Ryan took over. I loved her dearly but she didn't get spice at all. I left soy sauce on the counter. "Hint, hint."

"I'm not cooking Chinese," she replied, and put it away.

"Mix and match. Live a little. Go for the gusto."

"I like the way things taste naturally." Her eyes traveled down my body.

I didn't stop blushing until the pasta was done boiling.

She kept her schedule taped to the inside of one of her binders. The plastic-covered index card detailed class hours, study hours, track and weight training. A similar card, highlighted in yellow, had track meet dates and times. I'd been tempted to watch her practice, but I was too much of a coward to go to the track. The thought of all those athletes intimidated me. Also, I was afraid that Ryan would jump a hurdle and just keep going. I was afraid that, sooner or later, she'd outdistance me, run off and leave me behind. I took another peek at her schedule. Sunday wasn't listed but I knew that that day was reserved for church.

"What do you do on Saturday night?"

"If I'm home, I go to Bible study."

I wanted to break her routine. It was a perverse desire, but I wanted to know that I'd made an impact on her besides grades.

"Spend the night," I suggested one Friday as the candles burned low.

"I'd like that."

But she was gone again in the morning, backpack, books and jacket. Another lover might have invited her to leave a toothbrush. I wanted her books. We'd fallen in love over them and I let it bother me. I raised the subject again the following week.

"You're a great teacher," she said.

An emotion surfaced, hot disappointment. "Is that all?"

"All that stuff you taught me about how to organize my papers, using examples to support my points. It really paid off during midterms."

"Glad I could help," I croaked.

"But the really useful thing is the way you always know what the teachers want. That's such an excellent trick. I wouldn't get all that — what do you call it? Nuance. I don't think I'd get that on my own." We'd finished studying and she was packing up. "I'm really grateful, Andrea. Now I'll have a chance to get into seminary, a chance to do what I really want."

"Ryan." My mouth was a dry stream bed, my teeth dull bits of gravel, my tongue as lifeless as a withered snake. *Wimp,* I scorned myself. Anger forced saliva into my mouth, stinging tears to my eyes. Did she think she could pay for a few tutoring sessions, make love to me and walk out? Not without a fight. "Ryan, are you breaking up with me?"

She gave a startled laugh. "No, silly." She frowned. "Do you want me to?"

"No." My tongue died again.

She caught me up and forced a kiss onto my lips. Always, when we kissed, her mouth was soft. It might be shallow or deep, but always tender. Now I felt her teeth, as though she'd bared her lips. I couldn't breathe and had no choice but to open my mouth. As soon as I did, her tongue was in. I stopped resisting. She must have felt me soften because she did, too. Eventually, I tipped my head to meet her eyes.

"How can you doubt that I want you?" she demanded.

My voice was thin, as though it had been some distance away and was just coming into hearing range. "I know you want me, think you love me."

She shook me a little. "I do love you."

I nodded. "I believe you."

"What then?"

"I want you to stay —"

Her arms loosened. "Do you want to live together?"

It wouldn't work. As much as we desired each

other, my apartment was too small. Her dorm room was out of the question. I needed privacy, and Ryan, so disciplined, thrived on her busy timetable. But whether we lived together or not, the real problem was the fact of her coming and going.

I went to the window and looked down. My upstairs apartment was in an old house, far enough from campus for affordable rent. It lacked off-street parking, an inconvenience during snow storms when cars left on the street were apt to be towed. I'd saved enough last summer for a secondhand hatchback. When it snowed, I left it at the elementary school a few blocks up and retrieved it before the school buses returned.

Ryan was standing behind me, and I could sense her frustration. She didn't understand my fear and so could do little to allay the tension. My life, I thought, as I stared at the unwelcoming streets, was scheduled around inconveniences, like how to pay the rent and where to park my car, much as Ryan's was dictated by track and field and church. It occurred to me that her dorm was some distance away and she took the trouble to drive over every evening. Just because her car was newer didn't mean she had an easier time finding parking.

But it wasn't her car I was jealous of. I envied her the people in her life, most of all those whom she seemed to take for granted — the parents she saw every Sunday, the teammates she trained with every day. They were too numerous for me to compete with them all.

If I made a list of things to do each day, she would be the first and last thing I wrote. *Say goodnight to Ryan. Kiss her good morning.* And there would be precious little else, besides school, to say or do. And, although I knew I occupied the same slots on her list, there were many more people and events taking up her time.

She was standing close enough that I could feel her warmth. In a moment she would reach for me, try to soothe my restiveness. What she didn't know was that she was the source as well as the cure. When she was with me, the loneliness went away. Without her it echoed, redoubled, resounded. How could I ask her to do more, stay with me more than she already did?

Be with me. Fill me so the emptiness doesn't ache inside. The request never left my lips. How could she answer except to say, *I can't.*

I turned and wrapped my arms around her. "I love you. So much it hurts."

She took me to bed but we didn't make love. At dawn, when it was time for her to go, when her schedule told her it was time to run, she gave me a squeeze. "Are you awake?"

"Yeah."

"Are you still sad?"

"Only a little."

"I love you," she said. "Even when I'm not here. It doesn't stop because I go away. Can you try to remember that? Even when I'm somewhere else, I still love you."

It surprised me that she'd guessed so much. "Thanks." Her hands were under my flannel shirt and this time her caresses had a purpose. My nipples began to tingle. "You'll miss your run."

"Haven't you heard of a quickie?"

She tickled me until I laughed, loved me until I gasped, groaned, collapsed.

I reached for her as she pulled her clothes on. "What about you?"

"I'm going to do a fast run and take a cold shower. Then I'll grit my teeth until I come over tonight."

I bit her shoulder before she put her shirt on. Tender again, we kissed goodbye. I lay back, almost content for once in my life.

Chapter 5

My parents, non-believers though they were, had tried to do right by my Jewish education. Every Saturday on his way to the law office, over my protests, Dad had driven me to Sabbath school. Julia was excused from religious study. Mom had taken her to tennis tournaments instead.

At the synagogue, the children swirled apples in honey to celebrate a sweet new year. At Passover we spread horseradish on matzah and dipped parsley into saltwater, shedding tears over the bitterness of slavery. Grandma and I were the only ones in the family acting like Jews. At religious school, the other girls wore dresses and tiny studs in their pierced ears. Julia would have fit right in. I insisted on wearing corduroy pants and having my hair cut so short that strangers thought I was a boy. I watched the lithe, pale girls with their jewelry and braided hair and suspected my parents of foul play. They didn't care if I learned Scripture. This was Jewish charm school.

The year I was eleven, I licked my fingers clean of the Rosh Hashanah honey and refused to go back. On Saturday morning I stepped out of my pajamas, pulled on my corduroys and favorite brown and green striped T-shirt and crawled into bed with Jack London's *The Call of the Wild*. Mom, then Dad, hollered at me, but I put the covers over my head and wouldn't budge.

"Let her alone," Dad bellowed at Mom. "Let the kid sleep late if she wants to."

Mom was in my room. "Andrea, we paid good money to send you to the synagogue school."

"So save it."

"Your father will be at the office all day and Julia has a match. You can't stay home alone."

"Take me to Grandma's."

She sounded angry. "Get dressed."

I threw off the covers and sat up. Her mouth compressed when she saw my attire. "Can't you wear anything but those tatty old jeans?"

"They're not jeans. They're cords."

Julia dashed into the room wearing a tennis skirt and anklets. The socks had pink and blue balls on the ends to keep them from slipping under her heels.

"I have to go. Right now, Mom." She looked at me. "Brush your hair. You look like a dork."

I stuck out my tongue.

Mom said sharply, "Andrea, get ready."

I brushed my hair and brushed my teeth. I heard Dad's car start. Mom was in the kitchen. I picked up the phone in my parents' bedroom and dialed my grandmother's number. "Can I come over?"

I took four library books. Mom drove in tight-lipped silence.

Julia whispered, "Brat. You're making me late."

Grandma had opera on the radio. I ran in, hopped up on her high sofa and read until it was time for lunch. Then we walked around the corner to the delicatessen and ate corned beef sandwiches. I squirmed in my seat, trying to pay attention to the people and conversation. She ordered me a cherry 7UP, drank coffee and chatted with the old men and women — politics I didn't understand about a place I couldn't go because I didn't speak Hebrew. Every now and then the voices around me slipped into Yiddish, words that meant, *Don't let the child hear.* But they didn't mind my being there. They asked my name, pinched my cheek and went back to their bagels and whitefish. I was neither included nor criticized, and their way of ignoring me seemed to say, *When you're older there will be time enough for you to learn and worry.*

Until winter vacation, I went every Saturday. When I thought back on that time, I realized that Grandma must have given up the morning synagogue service, staying home to keep me company while I lay on her couch with my face in a book. I learned to relax a little on Saturdays. Dad was at his office preaching sermons to his clients. Mom was with Julia, watching from the sidelines, chanting and swaying and praying for match point. But I was safe in the steamy delicatessen, delighted to be in a world where grown-ups worried in a foreign language so I didn't have to.

A week before finals, Ryan was in my apartment watching me cook. I was making bean burritos with two kinds of cheese and was busily chopping my way through peppers, onions and cilantro.

"What's all that?"

"Salsa." I sprinkled in chili powder.

"Don't make it too spicy." She hugged me from behind.

"Watch out." I was still chopping.

"What are you doing for the holidays?"

I put down my knife and pushed her away. "Don't you think we should get through finals first?" I turned my attention to the beans. "I'm going to do what every self-respecting Jew does this time of year. Get take-out Chinese and keep the radio off so I don't have to listen to Christmas carols."

"You're not going home?"

I whacked the stirring spoon on the side of the pot. "In case you haven't noticed, this isn't a dorm. It doesn't close for the holidays. This is my home."

She was flustered. "Sorry."

I wanted to hate her for having a family, for

being able to anticipate the holiday season with joy instead of dread. I envied her but I didn't hate her.

"Don't apologize." I handed her a plate of warm tortillas. "Eat my cooking. Let's forget the holidays, okay?"

"Sure." Her eyes were veiled. "For now."

All week long we studied intensely.

"B's are okay." Ryan looked up from her books as though she'd just tasted an interesting dessert. "But I'd really like to get an A. Just once, I want to write a paper exactly the way the teacher wants it, make all the right points in the perfect order."

"You already did." I took off my glasses and rubbed my eyes. We were working late. "That's what a B is — exactly what the teacher expects."

She raised her eyebrows. "What's an A?"

I grinned. "Original thought."

"You told me you get A's because you know what they want. What about all that nuance stuff?" She flung her pencil down. "Don't change the rules now, Stern."

She was anxious about finals. She only called me by my last name when she was tense.

"The rules." I counted, ticking off my fingers. "Outline your points. Give specific examples. Always build toward a conclusion."

"I know that," she snapped.

"That's why you got B's on your midterms."

"If there's more," she said icily, "don't you think you left it until a little late in the semester?"

"I just figured it out."

She got up and started to pace, then flung herself

onto the futon. "I can't believe you're doing this to me."

"It's not like I planned it," I said defensively.

"You're a tutor. It's your job to know the lesson plan."

When we became lovers, I'd tried to stop taking her money. She insisted; I refused. We compromised, and she paid me for one session each week instead of two, but she made up the difference by buying most of the food. I hadn't meant to let her down. But the last component, the inner secret lurking in my study habits had just bobbed into sight like a buoy. I couldn't believe I hadn't noticed it sooner.

I scooted my chair around. "I wasn't trying to keep anything from you. Until you asked me just now —" I broke off, thinking back. "It was what you said about making the right points in the right order. I just realized that's not what I do. It's almost like that," I said quickly. "But not exactly."

Ryan was sprawled on the futon. "Come over here. I want to strangle you but I don't have the energy to get up."

I said, "You have to deviate a little. If your outline is too pat, you won't get full credit. Take one point and go a little further. Make your own interpretation, give your opinion." Ryan was staring at me. "Don't do it too much," I cautioned. "You still need an outline. But if you make all the connecting points, you can be a little creative. Teachers like that."

She stood up. "All I ever tried to do, before I met you, was to say what I thought."

"You lacked structure. You were all over the map.

Now that you know how to organize things, add your ideas."

She limped tiredly back to the table. "I think I hate you." After a minute she looked up. "I didn't mean that. I've never been so scared about exams." She lowered her voice. "I really think I can do it this time. I feel hot."

"I know." We gazed at each other. To take the edge off, I asked, "Do you usually get verbally abusive before a big race?"

She tackled me out of my chair. We stumbled to the futon and fell, laughing. I was letting my hair grow and the long curls got into my eyes. She tucked them back. I started to kiss her but she didn't respond.

"What? Are you still mad?" When she didn't answer, I persisted, "What is it?"

"You get good grades because you know what they want, but it's not the same as what you think."

"You don't know what you're talking about." A small voice within me whispered, *Yes, she does.*

"The way you say it, you make them think it's coming from you."

"Don't you think a professor can tell the difference between her thoughts and mine?"

Ryan said quietly, "You're better than they are. You sell them on their own ideas."

"What am I, a car salesman with a good vocabulary?"

"I didn't say that." She reached for me but I knocked her hand away. She got up and began packing her books. "I thought you knew."

"You think I'm faking it."

"Well, yeah, kind of."

I turned and stared out the window. She could go or stay, I didn't care. She was on her own for finals. I didn't want to help her anymore. My little voice said, *She doesn't need your help.* I bit my lip but the tears had already started. I heard her set her pack down. I was still sitting on the futon. In the window's reflection, I could see her standing behind me.

"I thought you were the faker," I said. "When I met you, I thought you wanted to learn tricks, you know, to get good grades. I didn't think you cared about learning."

She said, "That's what I don't get about you. You care, but it's like you just do whatever to get the best grade."

"Isn't that what you do when you run?" I looked at her reflection. "You do whatever it takes to win."

"No. That's what cheaters do."

I whirled. My voice was thick because of the tears. "If that's what you think I am, then why are you here? It won't look good on your priest's application if you tell them your tutor's a cheat." She crossed her arms and didn't answer. "Make your point!" I thundered, but she already had.

The part of my mind that listened, assessed, but rarely got involved, said, *You sound like your father.* I heard Julia, clapping, and remembered how Dad used to circle me verbally at the dinner table. Julia's obnoxious voice piped, *"Andrea's in trouble."*

I'd always assumed that he won our arguments because he was more literate, with access to abundant knowledge and experience. I'd copied his style and mannerisms, his tone of voice. He could convince anybody — judges and juries most especially. As a child, my father's voice had been the loudest, the one most often quoted. I argued with him, but he always proved himself right.

My mind was racing, but the portion of my brain that stood apart had already come to a conclusion: *Ryan's right*. The rest of my psyche was up in arms, slapping together a fortress and a defense.

Ryan knelt in front of me. "The only reason I know is because you're such a good lover. That's when you show me who you are. When we're studying, you're so hot but you hold back. Not in bed, though." She smiled.

I wiped my face. "Maybe instead of finals I should sleep with my professors."

"Don't. I'd have to kill them to defend my honor and then I'd never get to be a priest."

I laughed, remembered I was angry at having been exposed and searched for anything to fling at her. My mind was empty. It was like going back to a classroom to retrieve a notebook, only to find the board wiped clean, the desks cleared. The part of me that hung back, the honest part, walked in. It was like two people in a house who habitually avoid each other, all of a sudden face to face. There was the bulk of me who faked it, and the tiny slice of consciousness who knew better. I wanted to let the small piece speak.

It took a long time because that voice was rusty. It felt like trying to connect old railroad ties. The pieces were heavy to the point of being immobile; they creaked and strained and refused to line up. I finally spoke in fits and stops, bumping and jarring while Ryan sat on her heels and listened, patient during my unburdening.

"It's easier. I can make the conversation go smoothly . . . if I want to. Or an essay. The words just flow. You —" I heaved a sigh. "I thought you wanted me to teach you that, how to make people . . . like what you say." I coughed the rest of the tears out of my throat. "I don't know if I can tell . . . what I really think."

I reached down and picked up one of her hands. She sat placidly, letting me examine the tapered fingers, square nails. I needed to focus on something other than myself. Not anything. This woman. Ryan.

I said, "My parents used to fight a lot. My sister and I fought, too. When we were all together, no one listened. I know how to win arguments, but it's not the same thing as being heard."

She moved to sit beside me and put an arm around my shoulders. I felt drained. Not empty, though. I was full of an indefinable emotion. It may have been hope.

"Don't you get tired of hiding? I mean, if someone doesn't like your opinions, so what?"

Then I lose.

Ryan didn't have to worry about being alone. She had her family, her church, her faith. All I had were good grades, and she was knocking them down like empty soda cans off a fence rail.

Make your point, Andrea.

I don't have a point, Dad.

No point, no excuse, no reason to live or be loved. I couldn't hit a tennis ball like Julia. I wasn't pretty like Mom and I didn't argue as well as Dad. My dilemma was pitiful — keep faking it and lose Ryan; get real and lose the rest of the world.

"Promise you won't leave me."

She held me. "I promise."

In the morning, I woke up alone but Ryan had left a note. "See you tonight."

She'd taken her backpack but her books were stacked on the table. I hugged myself and headed for the shower. Final papers were due in days. I had a lot of writing to do.

One night after finals, Ryan made dinner — spaghetti and zucchini. The noodles and the vegetables were limp. It amazed me that someone so vibrant could cook such bland food. When I thought she wasn't looking, I doused my plate in soy sauce.

We were relaxed. Campus was closed for winter break and we'd just picked up our graded blue books and papers. Official grades weren't posted yet, but it was easy enough to tell — finals carried the most weight. To celebrate, I poured Manischewitz wine.

Ryan took a sip and winced. "That's sweet."

I opened a can of 7UP. I'd done my own grocery shopping for the week. "Try it now."

She looked doubtfully at the fizzing wine and soda. "Won't that make it worse?"

"Trust me. I grew up on Manischewitz spritzers. It's the best way to drink the stuff." I offered a toast. "To the new scholar in the family."

She was trying not to make a big deal out of it but she couldn't help beaming. "It really doesn't bother you, does it?"

"To have tutored you so successfully? I take full credit for your good grades."

She'd still pulled a B in history, but her comparative literature paper was topped by the slashes of a boldly inked A. Her professor had written, "Fine effort. This work shows academic maturity."

On one of my papers, a disappointed teacher had scrawled a B plus. "You've developed some interesting points," the note read, "but without your usual insight."

"Of course she didn't go for it," I said when Ryan excitedly showed me her paper and I shyly showed her mine. "These are my thoughts, not hers. Hey, it's okay. I need more practice, that's all."

Ryan was getting flushed from the wine. "Come home with me for the holidays."

I felt a rush of love, but — Christmas with the Mann family? I pictured a decorated tree, candles in the windows, holiday cookies, wrapped presents, laughter and caroling. Church. Midnight mass. I said softly, "I'm not ready for that."

"Are you going to stay here?"

"Yeah." I took her hand. "Thanks for asking."

Chapter 6

I read quietly through Christmas Eve, keeping the lamp on long past midnight, and woke up early on Christmas morning. I fixed bagels and coffee and read some more. On the table where Ryan and I so often studied were a couple of new notebooks and a box of felt-tipped pens. The emotion that she'd drawn out of me hadn't gone away. If anything, since my grades had dipped, it felt stronger. I was beginning to recognize it as the urge to set down my own thoughts, in my own voice.

My grandmother's voice joined itself to the sounds

in my apartment — the gurgling coffee pot, the creaking pipes. *"Andrea, when are you going to write a book?"*

I whispered, "Soon, Grandma."

A Hanukkah card had arrived from Mom. I'd sent her one as well, our notes passing politely in the mail. This year, the same as last, I'd sent Julia a matted print. I couldn't forget the residential program, the blank walls of her bedroom. The last time I'd been to see Julia was during the holiday season of my freshman year. We'd waded through a mother-supervised visit, after which Mom and I had a screaming fight in the parking lot.

"You know, Mom, Julia might get better if you'd back off a little. And you can stop acting like I'm going to poison her drinking water. I'm not hurting her."

"You're hurting this family with your irresponsibility."

"Like what?" My voice was getting louder.

"You give no thought to what anyone else needs. You could have gone to a less expensive, in-state school. You're selfishly acting out, as always."

"If you think the paltry sum you're contributing to my education is going to save Julia, then by all means, give her the money."

"If your attitude doesn't improve, I just might. For once, I'd like to focus on what Julia needs without getting flak from you."

"What Julia needs is for you to stop telling her how to walk, talk and breathe."

"I simply can't go through this every time you come to visit. If you need help with school, speak to your father."

"My father made a good call when he divorced you," I yelled.

Curtains at the residential program fluttered and a social worker peered out.

Mom got into her car and drove off.

I took the bus back to school. Since then, I'd let the postal service deliver my holiday cheer. I hated it that I wasn't seeing Julia, but I couldn't risk another fighting match with Mom. I was afraid I'd hit her next time.

A month later, Dad had paid me a visit at school. He spent the weekend, slept on my floor and treated me to a nice dinner. It was his way of saying that I hadn't been abandoned, someone in the family still cared about me. He listened to me vent about Mom but didn't have any suggestions for how I could make up with her. He offered to help with tuition but I declined. I knew he'd drop hints that he'd given me money and I didn't want Mom to have the satisfaction of knowing I couldn't support myself. I'd had to apply for another student loan. Before he left, I let him treat me to breakfast.

He hadn't been back for another visit, although we still exchanged holiday gifts, usually books, which was our way of keeping each other apprised of our current interests. This year he was reading the English mystery writers. I'd sent him a book on Celtic mythology.

I made fresh coffee and stared out my window. New snow had fallen; the pines and bare branches were lightly dusted. Someone knocked on my door. I opened it to find Ryan, grinning and wearing a new powder-blue ski parka and royal blue scarf. Her eyes were pale-flecked blue, the color of robins' eggs.

She held out a gift box. "Happy holidays."

"Hi."

Before finals we'd agreed not to exchange gifts. She'd said, "Save your money. Don't waste it on material stuff." She'd hugged me. "You're all I want."

I let her in and said, "I have something for you, but it's not wrapped."

"Andrea, you didn't have to."

"I wanted to."

She smiled. "Me, too."

"You should be with your family."

"I was. All day yesterday. We had dinner last night and went to mass. There's nothing left this morning but tissue paper and cookies." She handed me a tin. "I saved you some."

I accepted the cookies and examined her gift. The thin box was wrapped in silver paper. The bow was silver and blue. I gave it a shake. No sound. It had been a long time since I'd exchanged gifts with anyone in person. Ryan must have gotten a good look at my face because she stepped forward and crushed me in a hug. I got the cookie tin out of the way but the bow flattened between us.

I disentangled myself. "Wait here." My gift was inside one of my new notebooks. "Close your eyes."

"I hope you didn't spend money you don't have."

"I didn't."

Late the night before, after I'd read until my eyes were sore, when I couldn't forget the holiday or the fact of my being alone, after I'd brushed my teeth, turned out the light and slipped into bed, unable to sleep, I felt the universe begin to break apart. Air receded, and then a horrible, undulating emptiness washed toward me.

As always when I felt the wave, I closed my eyes and concentrated on my body. One by one, I tensed every muscle — toes and calves, thighs and buttocks. I spent a long time making my abdomen tight and impenetrable. I clenched my fists and pumped my biceps. My chest was harder to control. By the time I managed it, I was breathing shallowly. Somehow, by this extreme physical effort, I was able to resist being sucked into the void. Broken fragments of space, like shards of glass, swirled around my bed. By sheer will I forced the emptiness to compact, like my muscles, until it was folded, layer on layer like a piece of origami paper. Finally, the vacuum collapsed. Air and the sensation of substance returned. I no longer feared that I was going to spin off the edge of my world like cyclone dust.

When I finally fell asleep, I dreamed about Ryan. She was walking toward me across a sea of broken glass, getting bigger all the time. I saw her as a towering giant, then I rose to meet her. I was also standing on the broken glass, but I was so tall and strong it didn't cut me. Nothing else happened. Ryan came toward me and we stood there, larger than life.

In the morning, before I made the coffee, I opened a notebook and scribbled a poem. It was short, only a half-dozen lines, but I tried to convey the power I felt in her love. I tried to tell her that her love was stronger than my fear. I was beginning to rely on the love, to believe in it.

I ripped the page out of the notebook. I'd meant to copy it. "Okay. Open your eyes."

She looked at me. "I wanted to tell you about this weird dream I had last night. We didn't go to bed until really late, after midnight mass. I dreamed that I was walking and I could see you in the distance. You were far away but you kept getting closer. I walked right up to you and you were writing."

I held out the paper. "I'll copy it over later."

Looking perplexed, she took it. She stared at it long enough to have read it through several times and I began to panic. I should have waited, copied it, edited it or something. What was I thinking? Maybe she hated poetry. Maybe it was awful. I should have bought her a picture, a book, a silk flower.

She folded the page and tucked it into her jacket pocket. "Don't copy it." Her voice was husky. "I want to keep it like this."

She stood before me, very big, very blue in her new outfit. Then she took off all her clothes and shivered in my cold apartment. I hadn't made the bed and she waited for me under the covers. When I joined her, I loved her as completely and powerfully as I knew how.

In the moment of her orgasm, she became translucent. I reached through the glowing heat to where I knew her heart was pulsing. I cradled her. At that moment she opened to me like the universe, but instead of emptiness and broken shards, I saw color — magenta clouds, gold-edged buttes against a cobalt sky, and a lake of molten silver. Water lapped under her arms, between her legs. She shuddered, and I claimed the world she'd made for me, a new universe to replace my empty one.

We got up as dusk was falling.

She said, "Open your present."

"We said no gifts," I scolded. "No money. You agreed."

"I can afford it."

"That's not the point."

"Open it. We can argue later."

I pulled off the paper. Inside the box lay a cashmere scarf and wool-lined leather gloves. The cashmere was muted tones of brown and green. The gloves had matching lining. I couldn't take my eyes off them, kept fingering the leather and running my hand over the soft wool.

"Ryan, this is beautiful."

"I want you to be warm. It's so cold outside."

"I'm never cold when you're here." I wrapped the scarf around my neck, pulled on the gloves. "It feels like getting a hug from you, like holding your hand."

"You're sappy."

"Thank you."

"Since you're dressed for it, let's take a walk." I tucked the new scarf carefully under my jacket. She loosened my collar. "Let it show."

"I don't want to get it dirty."

She pulled me outside. We walked through the deepening twilight, taking a path that cut through a stand of woods on the way to campus. Our boots kicked up puffs of snow. Playfully, I tossed a handful, but it was too light to clump together. She pretended to ignore me, but when we reached an open field she wrestled me down. We threw white mist at each other until I was out of breath, on my back, panting and laughing. I looked up at her, her eyes in shadow, the sky over her shoulder purple with the oncoming night. Her parka was silvery, snow-dusted, and her breath came out in steaming clouds. Her cheeks and lips were cold, her tongue warm. We hurried back to my apartment.

We ran a hot shower and stripped. Standing beside her under the spray, I felt shy. Her strength was so obvious, her height so great. The top of my head came only to her chin. She washed me and then stood still while I ran a cloth between her shoulders, down her back. We didn't make love, didn't even kiss, just took turns soaping and rinsing each other until our flesh was rosy — mine olive-toned, hers ruddy. Gradually, my shyness eased. Openly, we watched each other.

"You're better about this." She smiled.

We toweled off and Ryan tugged a blanket around her shoulders while her jeans dried on the radiator. I made hot chocolate and we crawled under the comforter. My new scarf wrapped my neck, the soft ends draping my flannel shirt. She sipped her cocoa, wearing the veiled expression that meant she was absorbed in her own thoughts.

"What are you stewing about?" It was a question she often asked me.

"I've never felt this way before." The steam from her mug didn't prevent me from seeing her eyes. The blue eggshell color looked fragile. "Not about anyone."

"You've had other girlfriends." I'd never asked about them, and I didn't intend to start. I harbored enough self-doubt without hoisting jealousy aloft.

Ryan said, "Those were like . . . partners at a school dance. When you go around the room once or twice because the music's good. It's different with you. I don't feel . . . separate. Does that make sense?"

"Yes." *Because I live inside you.*

I finished my hot chocolate and scooted down so that my head was on her shoulder. When I closed my eyes, I saw the world she'd made for me. The sun had set and the sky was purple, shot through with streaks of powder blue. She kissed the top of my head. Beyond the silver lake, a small volcano erupted in shades of red and orange.

After a while she asked, "Are you asleep?"

"Mmm. Almost."

"Will you hold me?" We shifted positions so that her head was on my chest, my arms wrapped around her. She said, "You make me really happy."

I could tell she was still privately mulling. I was the one prone to brooding, not her. "Talk to me," I invited. "What are you thinking about?"

"God. Does that bother you?"

I woke up a little. "Why do you want to be a priest?"

I sensed her searching for the words to explain her faith. "I see things," she said finally. "Ever since I was a child."

"Like . . . visions?"

"Not really. Just light. I was seven the first time it happened. I woke up in the middle of the night and when I opened my eyes, the room was glowing. It wasn't a shaft of light, or a figure. I mean, it didn't look like anything specific. But the whole room was full of this really amazing light." She hesitated. "I never told anyone."

"Not even your parents?"

"No."

"What about your priest?"

"Not everyone who goes to church believes in mysticism."

"How do you know it was . . . holy." I tripped over the religious term.

She chuckled. "I call it sacred. That's a better

69

word, don't you think? I knew it was a sacred light for two reasons. First, I wasn't scared. I knew it was real but I wasn't scared at all. The second reason is that it was the most beautiful thing I've ever seen. No one can imagine or make up that kind of beauty. It's . . . radiant." She paused. "I didn't tell my parents because I was afraid they'd say I'd dreamed it. They'd make me sleep with the lights on or take knockout drops or something. I didn't want them to get upset and start calling doctors or the Sunday school teacher. Isn't that funny? I was seven and I didn't want to scare my mom and dad."

"Did you see it again?"

"Every night for a week. It was Holy Week, right before Easter. Am I freaking you out?"

"Not really. My sister hears voices."

"What do they say?"

"To hurt herself. She sliced her wrists two different times, bad enough that she went to the hospital. The third time, she cut her neck, too."

I thought about the chaos of those awful years, beginning when I was thirteen, Julia sixteen. I remembered the silence at the dinner table, broken by her repetitive mumbling. Late at night, Mom and Dad took turns yelling. I remembered lying in bed, hands over my ears, while Julia screamed retorts. Only she wasn't fighting with our parents. She was having her own hellish dialogue with the voices in her head. Sometimes she turned her stereo up.

One night I woke up to the sound of a car starting. When I went into the bathroom, I saw the bloody washrags. For the next two weeks, the house was quieter. Dad stayed at the office. Mom ran errands and did the grocery shopping, all the usual things. I stayed after school, studying in the library, walking the long way home, even though it was winter. Some nights, by the time I got home, Mom was back at the hospital for evening visiting hours. She always left a note on the refrigerator. "Leftovers."

When I was fourteen, I started cooking. I began with the easy stuff. Spaghetti. Brownie mix. I asked Dad for more allowance and went shopping. Pretty soon I was making Spanish rice and Indian curries. Mom and Dad had lots of cookbooks. Mom had always cooked for parties, but Dad had taken over on weekends, serving hearty winter stews or, during summer, grilled seafood. Not anymore. Mom ate my leftovers, and it wasn't long before Dad moved out, but I didn't think it was because of my cooking. Julia was back in the hospital. There was no more yelling. Except for Julia, who talked only to herself, no one was talking at all.

In Ryan's grasp, my hands felt small. I said, "The last couple of times I saw Julia, my Mom had to supervise, like seeing me could push her over. Like it's my fault."

Ryan sat up, resting her arms around her knees. "Do you think she's crazy?"

I thought about the first time I'd visited Julia at the residential program, Julia's teasing me while Mom tried to keep us apart.

"Hey, Andrea. Will you teach me to read?"

"Andrea, say goodbye!"

Julia, asking for my help, not Mom's. All those tennis lessons Mom had given her, and my sister was pretending that I had something to offer, something she needed.

I said, "Without medication, Julia tries to hurt herself. Other than that, she's pretty smart." I looked at Ryan. "I'm not saying you're crazy because you see things. It's not the same."

"Some people get terrifying visions. Others have experiences that feel transcendent."

"Sounds like you know a lot about it."

"I've seen it other times."

"Oh. When?"

"Usually when I'm praying or when I wake up. Almost always when I'm by myself. It can be a feeling, too, like being bathed in warm light. It tingles." She said matter-of-factly, "I've done some reading. Lots of people have seen a sacred light."

"I thought that was a near-death thing."

"Not always. I'm sorry about your sister."

"Thanks."

"Some people are more sensitive than others."

"My sister has a chemical imbalance in her brain."

"Maybe that's what makes her perceptions extrasensory."

"How come you joined the church and she slashed her wrists?"

Ryan didn't try to answer.

We were silent for a while, then she said, "Andrea? There's another reason I wanted to tell you about the light. I've seen it when I'm with you. When we're making love."

Gingerly, I reached for her, touched her face. "I see things, too," I whispered. Haltingly, I told her about the world in my imagination — the buttes and volcanoes, the silver lake, the sky that was cobalt or purple or powder blue. "That's my favorite. The pale blue." She'd taken my hand, and by the time I'd finished talking, she was squeezing it hard. "Hey, let go. You don't know your own strength."

"Huh? Sorry." Her grip went slack and her eyes seemed unfocused.

"Ryan?" After a few moments she blinked, and I said, "You looked far away."

"I was there. At the lake."

"That's my imagination. I just wanted to tell you."

"It's my dream place. Silver and light blue are my favorite colors."

"I didn't know."

She said, "I can't control when I see my light, but sometimes I imagine a place where I can find it. I picture myself floating in a silver lake. The light is all around me. That's why the sky is so pale — it's reflecting the light."

My heart was pounding. Under the covers, my bare legs goosebumped. "Are you saying I invented the same place as you did?"

"I think you added the pink and orange. My lake is peaceful."

"We were making love."

"That's when I saw the light. But it was here, in this room." My doubt must have showed because she said, "When I saw the light, you were at the lake. They're connected. The light is real, so the lake must be, too." She said excitedly, "No wonder I dreamed it all these years. It's real."

"Ryan." I spoke slowly, as if to a child. "The lake is a figment of my imagination." Inadvertently, I flashed on it. Glassy ripples marred the surface. In the distance, volcanoes were going crazy.

She smiled. "Count on a Jew to invent volcanoes. I'm Episcopal — quiet sky, no clouds. The orange is kind of shocking but I'm getting used to it." I stared at her. She whispered, "Do you get it? We see the same thing."

I should have known I couldn't handle so much emotion. Too much love. It was like an overdose and I'd gotten sick. I was terrified. If I could imagine something that someone else could see, then the world was in trouble. What about the demon beast that coughed dog's breath and drooled fear? What about the cliff, my father, the car wreck? At any moment the animal would bite my legs off, my family would plunge to their deaths, and the silver lake would rise until I drowned.

There was no way to have that power of creation and stay sane; I'd go mad. Ryan could handle it. She was strong, moral. She was going to be a priest. I was on my way to hell for having a vivid imagination. I'd join my parents at the bottom of a cliff or, like Julia, start slashing until I bled to death.

Ryan's arms were around me and I heard her soothing voice. "Too much, too soon."

A lamp was on. I said, "Shut the light." I was afraid to sleep, afraid of nightmares, but I was more afraid of the waking dreams. I clung to her.

"Andrea, listen to me. Go to the lake." Reluctantly, I let my mind drift toward the blue sky, the reflective silver. Almost at once, I felt calmer. "You're safe here." *There's not a demon in the universe that can reach you here.*

* * * * *

Afterward, I couldn't remember if she actually said those last words, but I heard them clearly. We developed a sort of code to talk about our experience. Ryan was positive in her conviction that the light and the lake were real. Although I hadn't seen it, I believed her about the light. For the first time in my life, I took it on faith — my faith in her.

The lake, I reasoned, stemmed from Ryan. When I was with her it was real, connected to her reality. Alone, it was just my imagination. My family dreams, my demon fear were my own inventions and unreal. It was an elaborate coping mechanism, but better than having to give up college and go insane.

Ryan began to describe things as "veiled" or "unveiled." She referred to the physical world as veiled reality. The lake was the realm of the unveiled. She called our love sacred.

"Anything sacred," she said, "is like a door to the mystical world."

At this point we were a couple of weeks into the spring semester — my junior, her sophomore year. Ryan was doing a lot of extracurricular reading. I couldn't handle large doses of religion, and she seemed to understand my limits.

She was at my apartment one Friday night when she said, "People assume faith excludes discernment. It doesn't."

She'd been late for dinner, arriving straight from a track meet, showered, tired, exuberant from her good performance. I'd made up my mind to watch a few practices, no longer afraid to see how good she was. Tonight, though, I'd stayed in to cook. I could tell she wanted to make love, but I made her eat and open her books. She didn't need tutoring anymore. I needed the study time more than she did.

I looked up from my reading. "Where did you learn to talk like that?"

"You used to sound that way all the time. Why do you think teachers love you? You make points like other students snap chewing gum." She smiled, pleased with herself. "You don't do it so much anymore. You're more okay with silence."

"That's because you're such a chatterbox."

She was cruising through her courses, writing papers with new confidence. I was the one struggling to give voice to my thoughts.

Recently, I'd asked, "How'd you get so good?"

"You taught me."

"I was only going through the motions. I didn't know — not really."

"You just never honestly applied it," she'd said.

Now I asked, "Are you going to tell me what you meant about faith, discernment, whatever?"

She became animated as she talked. She'd be a great preacher. She had . . . charisma.

"Faith isn't just a leap across logic. Spiritual people are aware of God. It's a personal experience."

"Um, what if you don't get it . . . personally?"

"There's always a connection, a way to know God."

I should have kept it academic, kept the topic at a distance, but I asked, "How do I find it? What's my connection?"

Her intensity pierced me. "Love. Andrea, that's the best way."

I was drained, defeated. I shuffled to the futon and collapsed, an arm across my eyes. I loved Ryan, more than I'd thought it was possible to love anyone, but she had a faith I couldn't match, couldn't really begin to fathom. When the night was over and the dreams were done, she had something larger than life to believe in. I just had her. I sighed and heard her chuckle.

I lifted my head. "What's so funny?"

"You're cute."

"I'm despairing."

"You're being melodramatic." She went into the kitchen and came back with a bottle of Manischewitz and a six-pack of 7UP. "I get a day off tomorrow. Let's get wasted."

"How can you drink that stuff?"

"A Jewish girl taught me."

"Don't call me that. I'm not religious."

"Andrea, it's the weekend. Stop arguing."

"Now the verbal genius needs some silence. Do you have a better suggestion?" I sat up, accepted a glass. Her lips were at my ear and I shivered. "Oh. Okay."

This time the clouds were the color of wine and the volcanoes spat fizzy red fire. When the tumult subsided, I floated in the silver lake, completely at peace.

PART II
To Love

Chapter 7

"Andy, we're on deadline. What've you got?"

"Running a spell-check. Hang on a sec." It was sort of true. I'd already run a spell-check and was waiting for a line to clear so I could send the document. My screen flashed a go and I hit the fax button. "All set, Cas."

"Great. Let's see it." I printed a hard copy and handed it over. He nodded enthusiastically. "Perfect. I'll get Dylan to jazz it."

Perfect, in Casper's lexicon, meant perfect for

rewrites. Dylan's way of jazzing copy meant adding text that read, "Hurry! This offer won't last!"

I said, "It's all set, Cas. I sent it."

Kevin Casper, my boss, smoothed a palm over his bald spot, a mannerism I'd come to recognize as a sign of irritation. He was a calm man who wore khaki trousers, Top-Siders, shirt and tie. I often thought he'd do better to keep the Top-Siders and lose the tie, or switch to loafers and add a jacket. As it was, he looked like he'd been caught in the middle of changing clothes. Short hair circled his round head and he wore round, wire-rimmed glasses. No one used his first name.

Casper's morality was his most remarkable feature, a human decency that included a saint's patience, a quality I regularly took advantage of. Ironically, it was his sense of fairness that offended me. He believed in group effort, team spirit. I reminded him, usually after Dylan had hacked my copy into trite pulp, about too many cooks, et cetera.

When I provoked him, he'd say, "You're a good writer, Andy. You need to get comfortable with your team."

I'd been on one of Casper's teams for four months, and each week I chafed more under Dylan's rewrites. The artists, Mack and Nancy, left me alone — ignored me, rather, in the way of artists who believe that advertising is nothing without art, that the words are a superfluous afterthought or a ploy to keep people looking at the pictures. In television, at least since the advent of the mute button, they were right. I had an edge in radio, which wasn't glamorous, and I held my own in magazines. It was my silent opinion that, although the pictures were pretty, it was my job to connect the dots between the product and the wallet.

Dylan, the senior writer, frequently penned, "Big savings! Limited time offer!" As the assistant writer, I took a softer, more complete-sentence approach, and Casper performed cut-and-paste editing, with the result that every ad looked and sounded air-brushed, easy to absorb, and stopped short of being original.

Casper supervised the artists and writers by lumping us into teams, hoping, perhaps, that we'd morph into something greater than the sum of our paychecks. His days were spent circuit-riding between the creative director upstairs and our cluttered desks.

At my desk, he pulled up a chair and cleared his throat. I was about to get lecture number three — obey your boss. Lecture number one was family values — keep the advertising clean and upstanding. Casper didn't like to use boobs to sell cars. Lecture number two was a variation on the golden rule — make nice to your office mates, and your boss will support your merit raise.

He began, "We'd get along better if you'd pretend to let me supervise your work."

"I know."

"Andy, have you ever cared about something? Really, deeply cared?"

I eyed him warily. Sensitivity-training was a different lecture. I answered honestly. "Yes."

"Good." He looked pleased, surprised. "That's the approach I'm looking for — less cynicism, more sympathy." He smiled, warming to his topic. "I know you have it in you. Let it show." I was getting his drift. He wanted to channel my energy into positive results. He said, "Let me have a little of your passion."

"No." He'd just inhaled, ready to transfuse me full of goodwill. My refusal blocked him like a blood clot. He gagged. I said, "I know what passion is. I know the feeling, and you can't have it."

In the spring of my junior year at college, I'd started watching Ryan practice. Her track and field events included javelin, long and high jumps, sprints and hurdles. Watching from the bleachers, I understood why she was so faithful to her weight-training. Legs pumping, scissoring over the hurdles, her body leaping, twisting over the high bar, or streamlined, perfectly balanced as she sent the javelin farther, so much farther than anyone else — her strength stunned me. I marveled at her power as she raced and soared. Watching her was nearly unbearable.

"It bothers me," I admitted.

"Why?"

The days were getting longer and she'd coaxed me outside for an evening stroll.

"You're physical, but untouchable. There's no way I can get close to you. It's inspiring, though."

"Why don't you sign up for a rec class?"

"No skill. No strength."

"That's what the beginner levels are for. To develop skills."

"I just wish I could get closer to that . . . perfect expression. But I don't —" *I don't know how.*

I was used to sorting my feelings as if they were walnuts — cracking the shells and scraping out the meats. When Ryan came into my life, she'd smashed open a whole bushel at once. But there was another crop, less accessible, and I was pondering what prying tool to use. When I watched Ryan race, I knew she was in that inner place where everything was broken open.

"You'll get it," she said.

"What do you think it is, exactly? And don't say God," I warned. "That's too general."

"It's when you're doing what you're meant to do. It's strong and peaceful at the same time."

"I don't think I've ever felt that way." I squeezed her hand. "With you. Not on my own."

Ryan slowed her pace. "One time in high school, I hurt my shoulder and couldn't compete. When I got back, my timing, my whole technique was off. The more I tried to figure out what I was doing wrong, the more screwed up I got." She stopped when we reached the field and sat on a piece of slab granite. Nights were still cold but the snow was gone. It wouldn't be long before the crocuses came up. She said, "I got so frustrated I almost quit."

I sat beside her. "You'd never quit."

"Coach sent me to the weight room. She said, 'Stop thinking.' That was it. That was her instruction. When I got on the field she said, 'Throw. Don't think. Throw.' I started listening to my body again. I'd been afraid to, because of the injury. My body knew what to do, though, and I had to trust it." She got up and stood behind me, massaging my shoulders. She did that sometimes when she wanted to say something personal, when she needed physical connection instead of meeting my eyes. She said, "When I compete well, nothing's separate. My mind and body are totally together. That's when I win."

"But you're giving it up to go to seminary."

Her fingers continued to knead, turning my muscles to mush. Only Ryan could make me relax like that. "It's the same feeling for me," she said. "When I run, when I pray." She kissed the back of my neck. "When we make love. It's the same perfect feeling."

"I feel it when I love you," I said.

I was in the library when it happened, so I didn't see the actual event. I always wondered how it might have been different if I'd stayed at the field, been down on the track. But I wasn't with Ryan when she died. She came to me.

I was studying in the library because my apartment had become a distraction. Every time my gaze wandered to the futon, I thought of Ryan and lost my place in my book, forgot to outline my assignments. So I left her to her track and field, walked to the campus library and spread out my papers.

The first thing that happened was that the temperature dropped suddenly and sharply. I looked up, for no reason other than the sudden chill. All around me students turned notebook pages, highlighted text passages, clicked mechanical pencils and punched calculator keypads, their concentration unbroken. Laptop computers chirped like toneless crickets. Then the noise faded.

Ryan.

I thought I'd said it aloud, but no one looked at me. She had her back to me and turned slowly. I wanted to ask why she wasn't at practice, but I could see that something was wrong. She had one hand pressed to her chest, and her face was full of pain and confusion. My chair was pushed back and I was on my feet, although I don't remember standing. I wanted to go to her but I couldn't make my body move. Whatever force had taken the sounds from the air had stolen movement as well.

It was several frozen moments before I absorbed the horror. She was see-through. I could see her organs through her skin, like one of those encyclopedias with glossy overlays — the top sheets peeled back to reveal tissue and blood vessels. I stared through her and saw her lungs pumping, heaving actually, as though she'd just run a heavy race. But where bright red blood should have flowed to replenish her muscles, it pooled, bluish and slack.

Stop it, I tried to yell. *Ryan, stop joking around.*

Her eyes locked with mine and she mouthed my name: *Andrea.* Slowly, her hand dropped away from her chest.

Between her frantic lungs, her heart lay quiet. It looked lopsided, as though it had been flattened along one edge, or maybe it was that one wall seemed thick, the other side too thin. It fluttered once, but the breeze that her lungs had stirred couldn't spur it to beat. While I watched, it shrank like a ball with the air going out of it. Her lungs drooped like tired wings and collapsed.

At the last minute I could move. Smoothly, and with surprising calm, I walked around the library table. The urgency that had been tormenting me — *what's wrong, my God, get help* — dissipated. She was like a statue, still see-through, her translucent skin bluish-gray. Her lips no longer moved; her eyes shone with tears that brimmed but didn't fall. There wasn't enough life-force left to let her cry.

I knew she could see me. As I had done when we made love, I reached to her, then through her, and cradled her heart. Unlike the other times, there was no glimmer, no heat. I closed my fist, clutching, trying to pump the muscle, to force the blood to pulse. But my fingers opened, dry and empty — there was nothing left to grasp. The wetness of her life, like the warmth, had evaporated.

I searched her face. *Tell me. What can I do?* Slowly, almost imperceptibly, she shook her head. The empty place in her chest was closing. *Don't go.*

A moment before she disappeared, her eyes cleared. The last expression I saw on her face was sympathy, and it shocked me. It wasn't what I wanted. Why, at the end, was she feeling sorry for me? If she loved me, I raged in a split-second's time, then where was the passion, even lust? She was done with those; who needed desire in heaven? That thought surprised me, too, because Ryan had never talked about heaven, only her lake.

Damn you, Ryan Mann, with your eyes full of tears that you can't cry and sympathy I can't use.

She'd wanted me to share her faith. It wasn't pity I saw on her face, but her grief that she'd failed me. She'd needed more time, years' worth, to convince me. Eventually, I might have believed, but we weren't going to get the chance.

On that day during the spring season, Ryan ran

her warm-up laps and her heart failed. No one at the track could save her. At the hospital, the doctors couldn't either. Too late, they found the stretched fibers and enlarged portion of her weakened heart. Least of all, there was nothing I could have done; I hadn't been there, had only touched her spirit and watched her die.

Her family laid her to rest in a small graveyard behind a white-steepled church in her hometown, scarcely two hours from campus. She'd been a local hero and the whole community, it seemed, had crowded through the church doors. I waited outside, shucking my jacket when the morning's rain gave way to sun. The mud steamed and began to bake dry. The ground was soft enough, by then, for a burial. I waited patiently for the service to end, for the uncles and cousins to shoulder her casket out of the church, into the earth.

A latecomer hurried inside. As the doors swung open, I smelled the incense. On a nearby branch, a fat robin tweeted. I said, "Yeah, I know. It stinks."

I gazed up and down the road at the parked cars, lining what must have once been a horse path. I was already on the top step of the church. All I had to do was turn and enter, ask for and receive the rituals and comfort. Through the wooden doors, I heard murmured prayers, faint music, the indecipherable words of a hymn. The robin, who had been listening for worms, came back to his doorway perch as the clouds finished clearing. The sky looked like a powder-blue shell, delicate as a robin's egg.

I was watching the sky and crying when the church doors opened and the procession began, led by crosses and smoke pots, the coffin, then the mourners. They circled the church and streamed to the cemetery. I got off the steps and wiped my face, trailed behind. I cast a look back at the branch, but the offended robin had flown away.

After the graveside service, the crowd thinned. Cars started up and made another procession to the reception at the Mann family home. As I edged closer to the grave, I was approached by a tall woman with Ryan's freckled cheeks. I smiled, delighted to see Ryan's body, although her mother had a rounder, less angular physique. But the joy faded. Mrs. Mann wore a dark dress and a hat with a half-veil — attire befitting a funeral. A silver cross lay at her throat, but not the Celtic style that Ryan had worn. The square heels of her black shoes sank into the grass.

"Hello. You must be Andrea."

I shook her hand. "I'm sorry for your loss."

"Yours, too, Andrea. Ryan told us about you. I'm sorry we didn't have an opportunity to meet before." We could have, I thought, if I'd had the courage to go home with her for Christmas. Mrs. Mann asked, "Will you come to the house for the reception? Would you like to ride with us?"

She was looking at me with such sympathy that I began to cry. I couldn't bear it, not from the daughter, not from the mother.

"Maybe . . . another time."

Spontaneously, she hugged me. "Please visit. Ryan loved you. We'd like to get to know you."

She moved off to a waiting limousine. I glimpsed her family — the solid man who must be the father, and a large-boned girl at the beginning of adolescence. Brittany, I guessed. She was clutching a medal, one of Ryan's track awards, perhaps.

I kept my head bowed over the grave until the cars were gone, then sat on the church steps, the doors already closed, until I'd finished crying.

The university held a memorial service at the field house. A few of Ryan's teammates approached me, familiar faces from the workouts, a few of whom, given time, might have become friends. There were a lot of teary women I didn't know, and I wondered bleakly if some of them had also been her lovers. They meant nothing to me.

After the memorial, campus life moved on, without Ryan and without me. At my apartment, I boxed my books and got a few dollars for them at the used-book store.

"They're worth more if you'll take credit," the clerk said.

"Cash, please."

The stuff I'd left in the library was still there, or in the lost-and-found. I hadn't gone back.

When the vision I'd seen had faded, I'd found myself standing, arm outstretched, in front of the study area. A few students were staring at me. I didn't know how long I'd been there. I was pretty sure I hadn't said anything. I didn't scream, although I wanted to. I just walked out. It happened, from time to time, that someone lost it in the library. The pressure and all. But I didn't create a disturbance, so no one gave my odd behavior a second thought.

I didn't bother with paperwork, didn't notify my teachers. I sold the futon, broke my lease and withdrew my meager savings. My sparse wardrobe fit into a couple of suitcases. The pots and pans and spices went into a box, and all of it fit easily into my hatchback.

I'd been on schedule to graduate early. If I'd stayed through the rest of spring and registered for the fall semester, I could have completed my courses and had my undergraduate degree by Christmas. I'd been thinking about taking a year off, working to save money while waiting for Ryan to finish. We'd talked about attending graduate schools close enough for us to spend weekends together — seminary for her, a writing program for me. The last bag of trash I'd cleared out of my apartment had been stuffed full of catalogues, applications, financial aid forms and my half-used writing notebooks. I was done with New Hampshire. I got on the interstate and headed south, back to Massachusetts.

Chapter 8

Boston was an expensive city and I shelled out for a grubby studio apartment. But it was far enough from Worcester, my hometown, that I didn't have to deal with my parents. I wasn't ready to face them, explain my loss. I didn't want to tell them I'd dropped out.

For a long time, school had sheltered me. Bit by bit, Ryan had eased me out of my skinny cocoon, introduced me to her teammates, my neighbors. Eventually, she'd have taken me home to meet her family. I hadn't realized all the fronts on which she'd had me moving, expanding.

In her sudden absence, my life felt like a failed airlock in a horrible science fiction movie — the guts of the ship blown into space, everything valuable tumbling away, irretrievable. Within me, the cold vacuum descended. Every feeling became an icy shard. So I kept my muscles tight, compacted. I folded myself flat, like a cardboard carton, and tried to keep the emptiness from taking over.

I got a job writing filler for a conservation newsletter. My résumé said that I'd attended Durham University. No one bothered to ask if I'd graduated. When the newsletter went broke, I got hired at a fishing magazine.

I spent the evening before my interview reading back issues. It was a regional, low-brow forum featuring local travel and tips on gear. The jargon tripped me up but I kept reading. At the interview, I produced an essay, also drafted the night before, in which I described cold streams and the shared enjoyment that comes from fishing all day without ever having to speak to your companion. They put me to work writing filler.

My inexperience showed soon enough. The editor, a long-haired Norwegian named Jan, tossed an inked-over draft onto my desk. My gut clenched. Rent was due.

"Andy, what's your favorite saltwater rod?"

"Um —"

"Tell me the difference between a wet fly and a dry fly."

"Um —"

"In other words, you wouldn't know a largemouth bass if it hopped into the boat and sucked your tit."

"I make it a point to know who's sucking my tits."

He guffawed. "The last two writers who worked for me were flunkies from the tournament circuit. They knew all the pros by name but they couldn't string together an adjective and a noun." He edged a hip onto my desk. He wore his jeans too tight and they pulled across the crotch. "Fishing gear is essentially the same year after year. Maybe the rods get a little lighter, more sensitive." He dangled a folder in front of me. "This is a press kit from a company that has a new line of fly rods. Do you think you can figure out what that means and make it sound exciting?"

"Sure."

"You're still on probation. Do your homework."

I got a subscription to a better fishing magazine than ours and started hanging out in sporting goods stores. I absorbed the lingo, learned that bass anglers use crankbaits and spinnerbaits, and what kind of flies catch trout or salmon. At the office, I made frequent trips to the water cooler and eavesdropped on the big-game braggarts, the catch-and-release fanatics. The legwork paid off and my drafts came back with fewer corrections.

At Christmas I received a card from Ryan's mother. It had been forwarded via the campus financial aid office. I'd notified them, and the bank that held the promissory note on my student loan, but I hadn't left instructions with the post office. I hadn't given a forwarding phone number, either. It seemed that my parents had also been in touch with the school, probably when their attempts to contact me at my old address had failed. When their greeting cards arrived, I sent them back unopened. I didn't want faked cheer from my family. They had no clue what I was going through and I wasn't ready to let them in on it. I hadn't even come out to them yet. I wanted to get a little mourning out of the way first.

Mrs. Mann's card wished me peace and renewed her invitation to visit.

I waited until after the holidays, until the worst part of the season was over, then placed the call.

It sounded like her but I asked anyway. "Mrs. Mann, please. This is Andrea Stern."

"Hello, Andrea. I'm so glad you called."

"Thank you for the card."

"How are you, dear? Will you come for a visit?"

On Saturday, the first weekend after the new year, I filled my gas tank and headed back to New Hampshire. It had been a cold, dry fall and there was no snow on the frozen ground. Fields were brown, crusty with frost. Horses wore quilted blankets as they grazed.

Ryan's family lived in New Hampshire's heartland, a region that swelled in the summertime with boaters and tourists. As I drove through the wintry day, I glimpsed kerosene-heated trailers littering the side roads, roped in by laundry lines. Lakes nestled between the mountains like chicks in a wooded nest, ringed by a pine forest.

It took longer to get there than I had allowed for. Although I was late, I pulled off the road at an overlook and gazed at the magnificent lakeside view.

There was no one plying the magnifying scopes with quarters, and I wasn't tempted to waste the change, had no desire to pick apart the trees from the distant cabins. A strong wind clapped my shoulders, urging me down the embankment. I braced myself and watched the gusts sweep harmlessly over the gray water. The sky was also gray, the shadowed underbellies of the clouds threatening to dump a storm.

While I stood shivering, hands balled in my jeans' pockets, my eyes began to play tricks. The view before me didn't change but I saw another picture, superimposed. The lake began to shimmer, as though the clouds were full of sunlight, not snow. On the horizon the mountains turned orange, as if at sunset, although it was only late morning. I blinked and the overlay became reality. For a moment, I was looking at Ryan's lake. By mistake I stared too hard and blinked again, not wanting to, and lost it. The water lost its sheen and all around were ordinary mountains. But what I'd seen left no room for doubt.

This was Ryan's.

I sat in my car until I stopped trembling, then drove on.

Thankfully, when I got to the Mann home, it was still too early for lunch. I accepted tea, which Mrs. Mann served in the sitting room. A sliding door opened onto a deck.

"You have a beautiful home," I murmured. *And a view that inspired your beautiful daughter.*

"It's even lovelier in summer," she said. "When the water's blue and full of boats. Do you like sailing?"

"I've never done it."

"Well, we'll have you for a visit when the boat's in."

I sipped my tea and set the cup on the saucer without too much clanking. Was Mrs. Mann making small talk, or was it possible she didn't know that Ryan had preferred winter's empty, silvery lake? And what did she need with me? I was a poor choice for a surrogate child — an unfashionable Jew, short and frail where Ryan had been Protestant, tall and strong. And in love with me.

Around the polite smile on her lips, I saw the question. If I spent days in her home, a month, if I returned season after season for boating and barbecues, she'd never ask it, although I could see it as clearly as her lipstick. It was a facial tic, a prick of tears when she thought of Ryan, a tremble in her hands when she poured the tea.

She'd taken the trouble to locate me, had bothered to send a card and ask after my well-being. Because she sensed that I knew Ryan in a way she didn't — not as a parent knows the flesh they bathe and clothe, but as a lover knows the skin and how to make it glow. She missed Ryan terribly and wanted to feel, through me, her affection. She sought a glimpse of what I'd felt when Ryan's love had filled me. It was a horrible thing to ask, but I couldn't blame her because she didn't know she had.

She ventured, "Ryan shared everything with us. I know that many gay children keep their lives a secret for fear of hurting their parents, or of being hurt, even condemned. Ryan's openness was a gift."

It sounded like Mrs. Mann had been going to support groups for parents of gay kids. I said, "Ryan was lucky. She really loved . . . she was devoted to you, to her whole family." I saw the glint of tears and prodded myself. *Keep going, Stern. Do it for Ryan. Do it because this is her mother and they loved each other.*

The large man I'd seen at the funeral walked in. I stood up, bumped my teacup and dabbed ineffectively at the wet spot.

Mrs. Mann said, "Ben, this is Andrea, Ryan's friend."

Lover, I silently amended. No matter how many groups parents went to, that word was a tongue-twister. He gave me a handshake, a gruff hello. Brittany ran into the room, stopped when she saw me.

"Hi, Brittany. I'm a friend of Ryan's."

"Ryan's with God."

"I knew her at college. I used to watch her practice, and she told me how much she liked running with you."

She stood, legs apart, hands on her hips. Her body hadn't finished the transition from child to woman. The coming year would bring height. She already had Ryan's confidence. She said, "I have her medals."

I kept the huskiness out of my voice. "I'm glad you're taking care of them."

She turned to her father. "It's lunchtime."

He looked helplessly at his wife, and Mrs. Mann asked, "Will you join us?"

"I can't stay. It was nice meeting you, Mr. Mann."

"Brittany, help Dad with the sandwiches while Andrea and I finish our visit."

Ryan's little sister escorted her father from the room. It shamed me to remember that I'd been jealous of Ryan's time away from me, the time she spent with these people.

"More tea, Andrea?"

"No, thank you." I took a breath and tensed, as if I were about to walk outside and jump into the icy water. I moved to the window.

"She loved this view," Mrs. Mann said softly.

I said, "She told me how much it meant to her. I mean, she described the lake. I think it's why she always came home on weekends — to be with you and go to church. Her family, the church, this lake, they were all part of her faith. She, um, felt . . . God's presence . . . when she was here."

When I turned, I saw the tears on her cheeks. I looked out the window again to give her time to compose herself. But she was braver than that. Of course she would be, being Ryan's mother.

She gripped my arm. "Ryan said you had a special quality, a way of . . . understanding. Thank you, Andrea. I had no right to ask that of you. I didn't realize . . . I'm very grateful," she finished. As she showed me out, she said, "I would never presume that Ben and I could become as parents to you. But if you ever need anything, anything at all, you can come to us. It's what Ryan would have wanted."

"Thank you, Mrs. Mann."

"Call me Margaret." She hugged me.

Ryan had known, in spite of my insistence to the contrary, how much I craved family. It was too bad

I'd lost her, and the chance to really get to know the Manns. Maybe I could have gotten used to Episcopalian in-laws.

Winter gave way to spring, and a sense of expectation, fresh as new paint, permeated the office. The fishing season was upon us and as Friday afternoons grew warmer and longer, desks emptied earlier. On Monday morning, only the doughnuts didn't tell tall tales.

I was one of only two women working for the magazine, the other being Jan's current secretary. Jan was an arrogant, self-absorbed boss who had a hard time keeping administrative help. As the warm weather prevailed and the travel writers disappeared for longer periods, I had the office largely to myself. My own workload was steady — the press kits kept coming and I was writing features on gear. Jan was also giving me other writers' copy to edit. The jargon had become second nature, and I'd hit on the right tone. He accepted my pieces without complaint.

On a quiet Friday afternoon, I passed Cindy, the secretary, on my way to Jan's in-box.

"Hi, Andy. Jan's gone for the weekend."

"This isn't due until next week."

"He doesn't let you do any field writing, does he?"

"You mean send me out to stand in snow-melt wearing leaky waders while the black flies are biting? Naw, he saves that for the grown-up writers."

She giggled. "My husband is crazy about fly fishing. He reads all your articles." She eyed me shyly. "He thinks you're a guy. You know, since it says, 'by Andy Stern,' and there's no picture. He says, 'Andy likes this rod,' like then I won't mind if he spends a fortune on it."

"I get as close to the stuff as the pictures in the press kit."

"Jerry can't tell." She smiled. Knowing that her spouse was spending money on the say-so of a woman obviously made the checkbook balance easier to swallow. "I heard Jan joking about it. One of the manufacturers liked the checklist you did for expedition fishing, and Jan got the idea of doing an 'Ask Andy' column. Except then he'd have to put your picture in."

"I use my imagination," I mumbled. But I wrote for Jan, using his style, and he was arrogant as hell.

"Well, you sound like you go fishing every weekend. The other guys do, but you only know it because they make such a big deal about saying so."

"Should I ask for a raise?"

She gasped. "Don't. He fired a writer who wanted more travel expenses. Besides —"

"I know. I don't really go fishing and I'm a girl." She looked relieved that she didn't have to spell it out. I asked, "Do you fish?"

"Who, me? I only took this job because I thought it would give me and Jerry something in common." I doubted that her strategy had worked. Jerry, most likely, still shoveled his corn flakes behind the morning paper and left her to Saturday's linen sale while he took off with his cooler and fly rod. She said, "He spends all of his time tying those bugs."

"Flies."

"You know what I think?" We were alone in the

office but she lowered her voice. "I think fly fishing is so men can do arts and crafts and no one will think they're gay." I laughed so hard I doubled over. I lost my breath and had to lean on her desk. She looked concerned. "Did I offend you? I mean, everyone knows you are, at least Jan called you . . . um, but it's okay and everything. I think you're nice." Her worried expression made me laugh harder.

When I got control of myself, I said, "Thanks."

"Are you sure I didn't hurt your feelings?"

"I haven't laughed in a long time." She thought I meant I hadn't laughed so hard. I didn't tell her it had been a year since I'd laughed at all.

Over the weekend I went to a sporting goods emporium, and on Monday I came to work armed with two beginner fly-tying kits, including vises that clamped to a desk, pliers, hooks, thread and wire. There was rooster hackle — dyed orange, blue, pink and green — peacock and mallard feathers, duck and turkey quills, sparkling tinsel and fuzzy chenille. Even dyed bucktail. The purpose of tying flies was to fool a fish into thinking it was gobbling a real insect. Tiers took great care in their craftsmanship, right down to the bug eyes.

At lunch, when Jan was out of the way, I set up the tools at Cindy's desk.

I opened the instruction booklet. "What do you want to start with, a classic brown trout fly or a woolly bugger?"

We wound thread onto hooks as if we meant to catch fish, and took turns reading the directions, our heads bent together, giggling hysterically when our creations fell apart.

She said, "If I get a good one, I'll let my husband

use it." She thought for a moment. "Maybe. If he appreciates it."

"Tell him Andy taught you. The guy who knows fishing gear."

She laughed and dropped hooks under the desk. I clanged my head picking them up. We forgot to eat our sandwiches but had her desk cleared and ready for business by the time Jan returned.

In spite of our attempts to keep our hobby clandestine, word got out that the secretary and the dyke had taken up tying. Jan, a blue-water man, made it a point to ignore us, but fly-tiers are predisposed to admire one another's work. As summer wore on and our skill improved, our fluff-covered hooks came up for critique. Between fishing trips, the guys leaned over our shoulders and gave advice. They began bringing in their own nymphs and streamers, and lunch turned into show and tell.

The best thing I could say about my job at that point was that it occupied my mind and paid the bills. I didn't have friends but I enjoyed my co-workers, except for Jan. I'd developed a weird and specific knowledge about fishing equipment, and I had a hobby that let me feel creative without trying too hard. Flies were tied according to specific patterns, so I wound the thread and chenille and followed someone else's color scheme.

During the hot nights, when the fan in my apartment blew nothing but stale air, I stood at my open window, ignoring the stench of urine baked into the pavement, and wondered how long I'd be satisfied living on the surface. How long, I thought wearily, before real emotion broke through like a hungry salmon?

Not long, as it turned out, and it was Jan who yanked me down.

He took lunch at the same time every day, and anyone left behind could be reasonably sure of an hour's uninterrupted peace. It was a stifling day in August when he came back early, sweating under the armpits. The office had air conditioning but the walk from the parking garage left clothes damp, spirits wilted. I rode the subway and was used to sweating.

The whole thing happened in about ninety seconds. Jan walked in, saw us working quietly and said, "Get that frilly crap out of my office."

Technically, we were in his reception area, at Cindy's desk, but we didn't argue. I began unscrewing the vises while she stuffed the feathers into plastic bags.

He circled behind her and I remembered thinking, *He wouldn't.*

He held off, in the end, didn't grab her, just brushed against her. She felt it and leaned forward, holding her breath.

He rasped, "Does your husband know you're getting it on with a dyke?"

I meant to hit him. I know because I set down the vise. I wanted to hit him with my hands. Not just for underpaying his female writer or sexually harassing his secretary, not just for being an unbelievable prick, but because it was such an obvious outlet for the rage that finally bit the surface inside me, searching for a hook. I broke my knuckle on his chin.

There was nothing personal at my desk, no pictures or mementos. The day was so hot I hadn't even brought a sweater. Jan had bitten his tongue.

He put his hand to his mouth and saw the blood. Cindy was still leaning forward; her frozen posture made me think of a fish trying to leap from a pond. I walked out, paid my subway fare left-handed and took the train to the medical center. I wanted to have my hand tended before I had to start paying my own health insurance.

They put a splint on and gave me painkillers, which I left in the bottle. For the next two days I lay in bed, my throbbing hand propped on a pillow, and stared alternately at the ceiling and out the window. I wasn't done with the grief, although I'd managed to stay away from it for a while. I thought of Ryan's family — Margaret's making tea, Ben's making sandwiches and Brittany's taking care of the medals.

I thought of my own family, whom I'd been avoiding. My twenty-third birthday had come and gone. Against the doctor's orders, I wiggled my fingers and yelped. I thought about my razor-happy sister. Maybe it was time for a visit home.

Chapter 9

I put it off for a couple of weeks, until I was
sure I could drive without passing out while shifting
gears. I used the time to make phone calls to rod
and reel manufacturers, trying to line up some
freelance work. I knew the product, the kind of press
material they used. But Jan had gotten to most of
them first, and my inquiries met with repeated
refusals. He was too macho to press charges, to admit
that a girl had decked him, but he effectively shut
me out of the industry. In the end, I got some dregs.
There were other people who hated Jan.

When I finally headed out, it took me a while to find my family. Since I'd been ignoring their correspondence, I hadn't registered the fact that both of my parents had moved. When I opened the door to my father's office, I was met by an unfamiliar receptionist.

"May I help you?" She eyed my splint, but Dad did criminal law, not personal injury.

"Is Sam Stern in?"

She looked blank.

A florid man I didn't know came out of Dad's suite. "Bunny, I need the Norberg case." He stopped when he saw me. "If you're the temp, you're fired. I need a typist with all ten fingers." He looked pointedly at my jeans. "I told them to send someone with a front-office image."

I said, "I got fired for doing physical rewrites on my boss's chin. The jeans are part of my ball-breaking bitch persona." I stared at his crotch. He stepped behind his receptionist. I sighed. "I'm here to see Sam Stern."

"Who are you?"

"Andrea Stern. His daughter."

"Crying to Daddy for the raise you didn't get?" He smirked. "Get out of here, kid. Stern quit five months ago and I took over his lease. If he doesn't want you to know where he is, hire an investigator. Bunny, give the kid my investigator's card."

"That won't be necessary." I backed out and stood in the hallway. Sure enough, Dad's name plaque was gone.

I found a fast-food restaurant with a working pay phone and began charging directory assistance calls, scribbling left-handed and trying to read my writing.

It was a weird feeling not knowing where my parents were, a side effect of my regimen of isolation. But it would have been worse, during the past year, to have seen them and acted like nothing was wrong. Now I had to start at the beginning, come out and talk about Ryan.

I charged another call and this time Dad answered.

"Hi. It's Andrea."

"You don't say? How are you?"

"Fine." My first instinct was to lie. I tried again. "I know this is unexpected, but I'm in town. Would you like to get together?"

I thought he might try to set an appointment for next week, but he said, "I'd love to see you. Where are you?"

"The burger place a block up from your old office."

"You didn't eat there, did you?"

"No. Why?"

"Rain forest beef. Boycott that stuff."

"Are you doing environmental law?"

He laughed. "Come on over and I'll feed you something healthy."

He gave me directions to a ritzy condo. The units were privately terraced, circled by a walking trail that led past a pool and tennis courts. I parked my battered hatchback in a visitor spot and prayed that no one would call a tow truck.

Dad grabbed my good hand and hauled me over the threshold. He was wearing a summer-weight linen shirt, safari shorts and sandals. The last time I'd seen him he'd been in a three-piece suit, chomping a cigar. There were no cigars in sight, no ashtrays, not even the lingering scent of tobacco. He'd lost weight and his hair was tied into a ponytail. It curled at the end, like mine. I was reminded that I looked like my father, now more than ever.

He said, "I hope you're taking comfrey for that hand."

"They gave me painkillers at the hospital."

"Comfrey's an herb. You don't want to mask the pain."

I wiggled my fingers. "No chance of that."

His condo had a small kitchen with an oiled butcher's block and wicker stools. Copper-bottomed pans hung from an overhead rack. Both of my parents were gourmet cooks, although Dad had only cooked on the weekends when he wasn't at the office. I remembered a few times when Mom and Dad had been in the kitchen together, wearing aprons and turning out soufflés. They should have opened a restaurant and stayed married. I wondered if, before having children, they'd lit candles, poured wine, made love.

The rest of Dad's condo was beige and plush. Vertical blinds were drawn back on a floor-to-ceiling window. On the sprinkler-fed lawn, a rabbit was nibbling lettuce.

"Is that a pet?"

"Shh. It's against condo rules to feed the wildlife." He smiled slyly. "It really pisses off the neighbors."

I sat on one of the kitchen stools while he plugged in a blender. He dumped in powder and a bunch of other stuff, started it whirring.

"What is that?" The churning contents were milky-green.

"Alfalfa, yogurt and vegetable protein powder. Wait till I add the banana."

The sludge took on a golden hue. "Dad, that looks disgusting."

He tasted a spoonful. "Perfect. Want some?"

"No, thanks."

He poured two glasses of filtered water and gave me a handful of capsules. "Here you go. Comfrey and calcium for your bones, and a multi-vitamin complex. Trauma is hell on the immune system, but we'll get you back in balance."

I followed his pointer finger as he showed me each pill, and I remembered how he used to lean over my shoulder, correcting my grade-school grammar. Before going to law school he'd studied English and Latin. Mom had also studied English and I wondered why, after the divorce, she went into law. Probably because she'd lost the man and wanted to keep the profession in the family.

I swallowed Dad's medicine and asked, "Are you retired?"

He got out a cutting board and began slicing cucumbers. "I gave up eyestrain, tension headaches and insomnia." He stuffed the cucumbers into pita bread and glopped on some algae-colored spread.

I said, "Dad, all your food is green."

"Smarty-pants. This is watercress and garlic dressing. You were always a finicky eater."

"How would you know? Maybe I just never ate your cooking."

"You didn't turn out too badly. I must've done something right." He set a plate in front of me.

I used a fingernail to lift up the pita and peek inside. "How come you left your practice?"

"I got turned on to vitamin therapy. You'd be surprised how many people are looking for alternatives to aspirin and blood-pressure medication. Headaches, even heart conditions respond to herbal remedies."

"You sell vitamins?"

"I sell health and I'm proof positive that the product works. Since I started vitamin therapy, I've lost weight, my cholesterol's down, and I don't need coffee to get energized in the morning."

"You lost weight because you're eating cucumbers instead of pot roast."

"I'll give you a starter kit. If you don't mind my saying so, you look stressed out." Dad had always been a natural salesman, selling juries on his version of the facts, his brand of bottled justice. He munched his sandwich. "How's school? You must be doing graduate work by now."

"I dropped out."

"You were always a gutsy kid."

"I'm not rebelling. I just didn't want to be there anymore."

He licked watercress goop off his fingers. "Making healthy choices is what it's all about."

"Dad, it's me, Andrea. You can stop talking in herbal sound bites."

He fixed his gaze on a point over my shoulder. "If there's something you need, I'll do my best."

Mrs. Mann had made the same offer and sounded more genuine.

"I'm not here for a handout. Aren't I allowed to come for a visit?"

"Of course you are."

I studied the vitamin jars lined up on his counter.

I'd dropped in without warning to gain the advantage. I hadn't wanted to give my lawyer parents time to prepare a case.

"Dad, did you ever fall in love again after you and Mom got divorced?"

"Your mother and I were never in love."

"Then why'd you get married?"

"Well, we thought it was love, so we married, had children, did all the things we were supposed to. But when Julia got sick, we didn't have the energy to keep going through the motions. Your mom and I don't have much in common."

He was lying, although he sounded earnest. Mom and Dad had made a great pair — at least, I remembered people saying so. What screwed it up? Dad's affairs? Julia's illness? Mom's ambition? I might have believed the whole mess was my fault, but I couldn't come up with a good enough reason. What had I done except try to be exactly like him?

I asked, "Are you seeing anyone?"

"I was dating the woman who introduced me to vitamin therapy. She broke it off, though." He grinned. "I did more sales in three months than she had in a year."

"Way to reach your goals, Dad." He laughed. I thought about Ryan and her races. "Did you know that the best athletes compete against themselves? They go really deep inside to see how good they can be."

"You were never an athlete, Andrea. That was Julia's domain."

"Dad, I'm a lesbian."

He stuck a finger in his ear; it took me a minute to realize he was adjusting a hearing aid. I hadn't known he wore one. "Is that why you quit school? To come out?"

"No." I'd never seen my father nervous.

He got up and selected a pineapple from a fruit bowl, thwacked it with a knife, severing the stem. He began carving vigorously. "I've always been very liberal."

"Are you still opposed to the death penalty?"

"Of course."

"You're murdering that pineapple."

He put down the knife. "When you were little, your mom and I . . . well, we worried. One of my colleagues was married to a psychologist and we had them to dinner. She assured us that lots of girls go through a tomboy stage. We thought we'd let it . . . run its course."

"You thought if you ignored it, it wouldn't happen. Thanks for the support."

"It's better for everyone now that it's in the open."

I hung my head. He thought I'd come over to come out. Coming out, with its goal of acceptance, was secondary for me, a prelude to my grief. Saying "I'm a lesbian" was as easy as "I quit school." The fact of my love was the easy part. The experience of it — the gratitude in knowing, the joy in expressing it, the devastation of losing it — that was what I needed to explain. I wanted to tell my family not that I could love, but who I'd become by loving Ryan, and how much of myself I'd lost when she died. But it was too much at once. I was reminded of our mountain hike, only this time Dad was the one who needed to rest, and I could sense the futility of trying to prod him farther, faster.

He'd managed to get the chunks of pineapple into a bowl. To change the subject, I asked, "Where's Mom living?"

"She bought a house in our old neighborhood. Almost as nice as the one you grew up in."

"Wow. She must be doing well."

"Real estate law." I heard his contempt. If a case didn't involve a courtroom, he thought it wasn't worth the retainer.

"How's Julia?"

"Well, from what I hear."

"I guess you take her vitamins and stuff."

"No."

After a silence, I asked, "You don't see her?"

"When Julia moved into the residential program, your mom and I came to an agreement. She filed for legal guardianship and asked me to waive my right to visitation."

It took a moment for what he was saying to sink in. "Mom pays the bills and you stay away? You're joking." The look on his face told me he wasn't. It was an old courtroom expression — a slightly pained look, as though he knew more than he was allowed to say. I didn't fall for it. "What about Julia?"

"It's better when divorced parents don't fight over custody, or in this case, treatment."

In retrospect, it was interesting that I lost my temper on Julia's behalf. I was frustrated, disappointed that I couldn't talk to Dad about my life, but he wasn't talking to Julia at all. I also wanted to ignore the voice inside me that said, *You're mad because you're not seeing her either.*

"You lazy bastard. You can't be bothered, can you?" I'd been away too long to come back and lay into him, but I didn't care. I said nastily, "Was Mom winning all the fights? I bet you hated it when she learned your legal vocabulary. Or was it greed?" I waved a hand, taking in the contents of his condo. "Vitamins earn you a nice living as long as you're not shelling out for psychiatric treatment."

He was still wearing his lawyer's look. "Go ahead and holler at me if it makes you feel better. It's what your mother wanted."

"She's your daughter," I screamed. I'd wanted someone to be able to stand up to Mom. I felt nauseous. From the comfrey or watercress, who could tell? I slid off my stool. "I gotta get going."

"Andrea, I know you're angry, but this was a family decision."

"We don't have a family. We have battle camps and a demilitarized zone where we meet and eat cucumbers and hammer out the tough decisions like who gets Julia. That reminds me, do you have Mom's address?"

He plucked a business card from a Rolodex. I glanced at it, handed it back.

He said, "Keep it."

"No, thanks. I have a good memory."

As I was driving away, I said, "Bastard." But I was already feeling more sad than angry.

I located my mother's name on a directory in the downtown district. Her office was in a shopping and business complex next to the convention center, convenient to out-of-town developers. Her secretary informed me that she was meeting clients and not expected back until four in the afternoon. I checked my watch. Two o'clock. I walked around the mall and bought coffee and a book. At four I camped in Mom's reception area, reading while I waited for her, just like old times. At five, when the secretary left, I had to wait in the hall. I sat on the floor, ignoring the stares that towered over me as polished shoes flashed by. Mom arrived at five-thirty wearing a yellow silk suit and toting a briefcase.

"Excuse me. Please don't block my door or I'll call building security."

I closed my book and got to my feet. "Hi, Mom."

"Andrea. What happened to your hand?"

"I broke my knuckle. Don't worry, it's healing. Dad gave me comfrey but I'm starting to think a glass of wine would be a good idea. Want to get some fettuccine and share a bottle? I'd offer to treat but I just lost my job. We can go dutch, though."

"Oh, Andrea." She ushered me out of the hall as more well-tailored business types walked by. "I have to make phone calls. Wait for me."

By the time she was done, I'd finished my paperback. We walked around the corner to the mall restaurant and Mom ordered a Caesar salad. My heart fluttered when I saw the menu prices. I ordered the same, although I don't care for Caesar dressing. I could almost hear Ryan. *Too salty.* And what was it with my parents and vegetables? Not a cut of meat in sight. I slathered butter on my dinner roll and ate with the dedication of one who isn't certain of another meal. Mom reached for the Promise spread and sniffed at the wine list. She ordered Chardonnay. I tried to muster some dignity and asked for the house red.

Finished with the menu, Mom put away her reading glasses. "You moved without giving anyone your forwarding address. I had to get it from the university. And you sent back my Hanukkah card."

"I quit school." Her lips thinned. I said, "I'm working as a writer. Um, freelance right now."

I helped myself to another dinner roll, trying to wield my butter knife left-handed. For a minute I thought she might reach across the table and butter my bread for me, but if she was tempted, she restrained herself. By the time our salads arrived, my mouth was dry and my arm ached from knuckles to elbow. I gulped my wine. Mom chewed lettuce, wiped the corners of her mouth without smearing her lipstick and sipped her Chardonnay. I felt sorry for her clients. Then again, they paid her to be as smooth as museum glass and just as hard.

"Why did you lose your job?"

"My boss was a prick so I punched him."

To my surprise, she smiled. Not one of those polite facial expressions that shop clerks dispense with change, but an honest smile that brightened her eyes and showed the gap between her front teeth.

I'd never thought about it in so many words, but that gap in her teeth was what I loved most about my mother. It made her smile seem wider, her features whimsical. I concentrated on it and forgot that she intimidated me, forgot, for a moment, that I was afraid she didn't like me. I kept thinking that if I stared at it long enough, a Disney character might slip out — a woman with starry eyes, flower-petal lips and a flour-dusted bosom.

Mom refolded her napkin. "I don't suppose you punched your father, too, during your visit?"

Since the divorce, Mom and Dad never called each other Faye and Sam. I was used to hearing, "your mother, your father." Mom's interest in boxing was a new development.

"I can't do much left-handed," I apologized.

"There's nothing more pathetic than a middle-aged man trying to have a second adolescence."

"You think selling vitamins is adolescent?" I was thinking about all the money he made, and how much he wasn't giving to Julia.

"He's got a girlfriend the same age as his daughter. He's having a midlife crisis and dealing with it the way all men do — with his penis."

"I think they broke up. She was twenty-three?"

"Twenty-six."

"Oh." Julia was three years older than me. I'd never heard Mom talk about sex. I'd never heard her say "penis."

She said, "I was worried when my card came back. I'd like to at least know that you're all right."

Dad had acted like I was on a grand adventure. Mom probably assumed I was homeless. As usual, my parents were polarizing the issue.

"I'm sorry I returned your card. I'm still living in Boston."

"Why did you leave school? Did you lose your financial aid?"

"It's kind of complicated."

Her tone of concern turned to impatience. "Did you drive an hour from Boston to Worcester and camp on my doorstep to eat a Caesar salad?"

"I guess the first thing I have to tell you is that I'm gay." She barely flinched. Hard-boiled businessmen probably stirred even less of a reaction. I said, "There are groups and stuff for parents, if you're interested."

"I'll look into it." After a pause, she asked, "So you left school because you're confused about your sexual orientation?"

"I'm not confused. I'm a lesbian. Why are you so obsessed with my dropping out?" I tried to read her closed expression. "I guess you wanted to have at least one daughter graduate from college."

"Leave Julia out of this."

"Pretty tough to have two kids fail to meet your expectations."

"I don't think of my children as failures. Please don't bait me, Andrea. If you have something to say, I'm listening."

I tried to ease into it. "It's been a hard year."

"For me, too. Last fall, Julia moved to a new program. The residents have private apartments and take their own medication, with minimal supervision. I had reservations about the independent-living model, but she's doing very well."

"Mom, that's great."

I was glad for my sister, and sad. A lot of time had passed, full of major changes, and I'd been absent. I'd blamed it on Mom, on the fighting. Then I'd blamed it on my personal misery. All the while I'd acted as if Julia were in stasis, as though I could come back at any time and jump-start my concern. I needed to make more of an effort.

I asked, "How're you holding up?"

"Fine."

"I mean it. How are you doing?"

Her lips trembled. "Mostly I'm fine, and I believe

Julia will be, too. Then there are days when I pray for . . . normalcy." She squared her shoulders. "I'm bringing her home."

"But you said she was doing well." I hesitated. It was risky to question Mom. "What about independent living? Isn't that the goal?"

"She's been looked after by strangers for too long. We can work on her goals at home. Dr. Meadows, her psychiatrist, thinks our family is ready for this step."

"She hasn't —"

"No suicide gestures. Not even delicate cutting." Mom was more facile than I with the language of Julia's illness.

"How does she feel about the homecoming?"

"She wants her own apartment."

"It sounds like that's what she has now."

"I can take care of her."

Why did my parents always have something to prove? "You are. I happen to know you're footing the bill."

"Your father shouldn't have told you that."

"Dad's a jerk."

"We agree on that much."

"Julia can live with me," I heard myself say.

Mom set her picked-over salad aside. "Do you think you can show up after all this time and cast a vote?"

"That's not what I meant —"

"This decision doesn't concern you. From the sound of things, stability isn't your strong suit."

I didn't want to lose my temper as I had with Dad. "What's the visiting policy?"

"I'd prefer that you didn't see her right now. Coffee," she ordered, as a waitress passed by.

"Two, please." I waited while our table was cleared. "Mom, I want to see Julia."

"She's about to undergo a major transition. She doesn't need any extra family strain."

"Is that what I am — family strain? If you think my being gay is going to flip her out, that's horseshit."

Coffee arrived and we glared at each other.

"Keep your voice down, please, and watch your language."

"Cut the motherhood and manners crap. You're trying to keep me from seeing my sister."

"As her guardian —"

"I can't believe I'm hearing this."

"I think a period of adjustment is best for everyone. In the meantime, I'll give you whatever help I can." She had her checkbook out.

"Is that why you think I'm here? To ask for cash?"

"Isn't it?"

"I haven't taken assistance from you since my first year of college." It had become a point of honor. "I don't need your money."

"Do you think you're an adult because you're paying your own bills? I've got news for you, Andrea. It takes more than that. I'm talking about commitment, consistency. Things you obviously don't yet know about."

I stared into my coffee. When I raised my eyes, I said calmly, "You have no right to say that to me. You think you do, but you haven't been a part of my life in a long time, either. Don't presume what I know or don't know about commitment."

She absorbed my words. "You're in a relationship. I'm glad for you."

I said bluntly, "I had a relationship. She had a heart attack. I fell in love with a woman and then I went to her funeral. So I guess I know what you're afraid of."

During the ensuing silence the waitress ducked in with the bill. I dug into my pocket. Mom took out a credit card. "Put your money away."

"I'm not Dad. I'll pay my share." I made sure I left enough for tax and tip. I said, "I know you think you're protecting Julia. But it doesn't work that way. If she dies, it won't be because I brought her a book or some brownies. Give me your address." She pulled out a business card. "Your home address."

She penned the information on the back of the card. "I'm sorry this hurts you, Andrea. I'm not saying it's forever. Please just give it some time." I had to stop myself from calling her a frightened bitch to her face. For all I knew, she'd get a restraining order. She said, "I wish you'd let me give you some money. You look thin."

"Deal with your guilt."

"A little advice?" I waited. "You might have more luck in the job market if you'd get some nice clothes and spend more than eight dollars on a haircut."

I said, "You might get laid if you'd lose the ice-queen power suit."

"You might be right." She smiled and the gap showed.

We sat for a while over our cooling coffee. Eventually, she'd let me back into the family. But I'd have to wait until she got a grip on her fear. She'd made up her mind to keep me away, as though she could limit the risk of infection, as though Julia were only in danger of catching the flu. I thought about Dad's decision to bow out. Mom was acting like she had the power to keep Julia alive. Dad was pretending she was already dead.

I got up before she was done with her coffee and waved her back into her chair. "I've got a long drive. I'll write."

She looked like she wanted to say something. I watched her search for the words and come up empty. As I was leaving, I glanced back. Her shoulders were slumped a little, her coffee forgotten. Because I wasn't watching where I was going, I smashed my splinted hand into the exit door. I walked up the street, swearing and crying and trying to remember where I'd parked my car.

Chapter 10

My hand healed and the freelance work dried up. When it came down to it, I could sell anything on paper, but not myself. It was the waitressing thing all over again — I got the orders right but inspired no one to leave a tip. I looked in my checkbook and then in the mirror. "Cut your hair," my mother had said. "Wear nice clothes." I grabbed a handful of tangles and remembered Ryan's hands holding my head to the pillow.

I didn't cut my hair but brushed it back and wore clips. I spent an awful afternoon in Macy's basement, trying to make discounts fit my body. In the end, I went upstairs and found a hawk-eyed salesclerk who outfitted me in slacks and simple blouses, sized petite. It drained my savings but it was a wardrobe I could wear. I spent the weekend with the want ads and wrote enticing cover letters. By the end of the month, I'd met Casper. He gave me a job, benefits, the works.

Once a month I wrote to Julia, updated her on my mundane routine and asked her to let me know if she wanted to get together. At the holidays, Mom sent a card saying that Julia was home and she'd show her my letters when she'd settled in. I fumed and stayed away. Mrs. Mann and I exchanged cards but there was no invitation to tea. We'd shared what we could. The rest of the grieving process was each to her own.

Before hiring me, Casper had sorted through my magazine samples. "How long have you been fishing?"

"I don't fish." He nodded as though I'd said something wise. "I learned as I went along."

He said, "There's a lot of opportunity here. This is a place where a writer can grow." It was my turn to nod. He explained the benefits and pay scale. I held my breath. It was money I could live on. "I'll need to check references, Andy."

I gave him the information. A couple of the sportswriters had agreed to help out, and Cindy had promised to keep any inquiries away from Jan. She was still tying flies and hinted that it wasn't as much fun alone.

"Let's get together," she suggested.

I told her my injured fingers were too stiff. I said, "I'll let you know."

After the interview with Casper, I muttered, "Nice try," and resolved to go looking for a ratty newsletter in need of filler. I was surprised when Casper called back, and I tried to sound nonchalant while agreeing to start immediately.

"You're fresh," he said repeatedly, adding that my writing showed potential.

Casper was a mentor looking for a mark. In addition to feeding and clothing his own children, he sponsored hungry tykes the world over. Every month a postcard from a no-longer-starving child appeared on his bulletin board. Casper helped out where he could.

I got comfortable with my work, read myself to sleep at night and watched my bank account begin to revive. One night I made a fist, then opened my hand, satisfied that I could at least put the trauma of a broken knuckle to rest. I thought about calling Dad, hoping my new job might impress him, but I didn't want to talk about vitamins. There were too many things wrong with my family that yogurt shakes couldn't fix. In January, my car died and so did the radiator in my apartment. The building super fiddled and faddled. The heat came on, then shut off. I scuttled, shivering, to the subway, and warmed up by lunchtime. When I sneezed repeatedly on the photos I was writing copy for, Casper sent me home. The heat was on, for once, but I awoke in the night with the sensation of being underwater. I slept sitting up, or dozed, rather, all the while feeling the fluid getting thicker. When I finally dragged myself to a crowded emergency room, an unsympathetic doctor demanded to know if I was trying to kill myself.

I said, "Not consciously."

He slapped a prescription into my palm. "The wind chill's below zero. At least wear a hat."

The pneumonia kept me down for a week, during which time I was delirious with fever. I dreamed that Ryan sat on the edge of my bed.

Hi, Andrea.

"Hi, Ryan." Her form was indistinct, glowing. She looked big and golden and very beautiful. I began to cry. "I miss you."

Shh. She soothed me. My flesh, shivering from cold, then raging hot, softened where she touched it. The shaking that had gripped my body subsided. She crooned, *You're not alone.*

Not true, I tried to yell, but a spasm of coughing choked me. I didn't see her hand, just an orange light over my chest. The tightness eased. I stopped coughing and closed my eyes. I felt sleepy.

Andrea, listen to me. I looked up and she was still there. What a weird dream. *Take care of yourself.*

Whose ghost was this — Ryan's or my Jewish grandmother's? I mumbled, "It's too hard."

The orange light was on my chest again. *It's in here. Everything you need. Andrea, stay hot.* Her eyes were very bright, not blue, but vibrant gold.

"Ryan? Is it really you?"

She nodded. *Remember the lake? It's more beautiful than we imagined.*

"I can't see it anymore. I can't get there without you."

She bent to me and my forehead tingled. I dreamed she kissed me. *The colors are different. You'll see.*

Before I fell asleep again, I noticed that my room was glowing. The air around my bed was filled with light. I convinced myself I'd dreamed that, too.

I asked Casper for another couple of days, then put a deposit on an apartment with a working furnace. I balanced my checkbook three times and wrote a humble letter to Mom. She sent a cashier's check by certified mail. I sent a thank-you note with a promise of repayment and no letter to Julia that month. Mom's money went for a down payment on a car with front-wheel drive. I made sure the heater and defroster worked. It was time to take the winter commute seriously.

I needed more clothes, but not from the women's rack. I went back to one of my hunting and fishing haunts and bought thermal shirts and an oversized hooded parka rated for the Arctic. The scarf and gloves that Ryan had given me were in my closet, wrapped in the original gift box. I kept it on a shelf where I couldn't see it unless I stood on a chair. I knew that if I opened it I'd cry, and I didn't want to indulge the tears.

But while I couldn't wear her clothes, I was doing the rest for Ryan's sake. Like my grandmother, she'd said, *Take care of yourself.* She'd touched my chest. *It's in here.*

When Ryan died, when I saw through her at the end, her heart had vanished. It stood to reason, my fevered brain decided, that I'd been given one in her place. Being the weaker one, I should have died, but she'd gone ahead and given me her heart. Now I had no choice but to listen to the doctor, stay alive and keep warm. It was the only way I could protect what was left of her love.

When I went back to work, I tucked in my blouses over thermal undershirts. It was a little bulky and I think it ruined the fashion line. Thankfully, the crud in my chest was breaking up. I was still coughing but I no longer felt like I would drown in phlegm. Soon I was back in the swing, sending copy to clients and getting Casper's go-ahead after the fact.

It was Friday, one of those dry, cold days in February when the breath in your nostrils freezes, when it's so cold that each nose hair becomes a crystalline needle. I pulled the insulated hood of my parka around my face and jogged into the building. I had just turned on my computer when Casper strolled in.

"Hi, Andy. You're here nice and early."

"I get more done when the office is quiet."

"I wish everyone had your work ethic."

I raised my eyebrows. "I thought I was hard to work with, a poor team player and all that."

He waved a dismissive hand. "That's attitude. You're like a cactus — scratchy thorns over tender flesh."

"Why, Cas, how sweet. I thought you liked me for my mind."

The top of his scalp turned pink. "That's just

what I'm talking about. I'm trying to tell you that I see your soft side and you start bristling." He waggled a finger. "It's a good thing I understand the artistic temperament."

"You're a saint."

"Spare me the sarcasm."

"I mean it. You're decent and fair. I know I'm impossible." I turned my attention back to my computer.

He pulled up a chair. "Why don't you drop the act?"

I took my time answering and fell back on a fishing metaphor. "Writing copy is like catching a fish. I give you the whole idea — fresh, wriggling, head and scales. But an ad is like a fillet. The client doesn't want the guts. They get the tasty part, served to look appetizing. If you got butchered day in and day out, don't you think you'd want a few spines on your back?"

He used the age and wisdom argument. "All young writers think their words are flesh and blood, but once the ink is on paper it's a separate entity. I tell all my writers, words aren't children. Don't get attached."

His pinup gallery of hungry orphans was beginning to make sense. Words and pictures trotted out the door, but the grateful postcards kept coming. I'd always thought Casper's cut-and-paste approach to editing was the result of his trying too hard to please everyone. Because of it, designs lacked clarity, a singular vision. Too often, I thought our product was mediocre.

"Remember when I asked if you really cared about something?"

"Leave it alone, Cas. I won't go there."

"I know." He sounded sad. "But it's the best place to work from. If you'd let yourself tap into it, you wouldn't have to keep your guard up all the time."

For a moment, I wasn't in the office. I was sitting at the table in my old apartment, the books spread out, and Ryan was talking about God.

"How do I find it?" I'd asked.

I remembered her intensity, her certainty. "Love. That's the best way."

I blinked and came face to face with Casper. "No way," I whispered. Under my thermal layers, I was achingly cold.

Casper said, "I really came down here to give you the big news. As of Monday, you'll have a new boss."

"You're leaving?" My voice cracked.

He smiled. "I'm going upstairs."

"Hey. Congratulations." A promotion was required to ascend the stairs. "What's your title?"

"Director." He was proud, and he had a right to be.

"What happened to Hanscom?"

"He's going to Mellen."

"Ouch." Mellen was the competition. "What about the clients?"

"We'll keep our share."

It was a quiet statement from a modest man. With a staff change at that level, the accounts people would be fighting wildfire panic. I thought Casper was an odd choice for creative director, and I wondered what the partners knew that I didn't. I'd never met his predecessor, but he'd been rumored to keep his phone on speaker-mode so his hands were free to pour antacid.

I asked, "Can you handle the stress?"

"I made these teams. No one knows what goes into your work more than I do. I'll keep the clients happy, and I'll make sure they appreciate what they're getting. By the way, I'm putting in for your merit raise. It's a little early, but I want the paperwork in place before I go upstairs."

"Thanks." Maybe Casper was the right man for the job after all. "This is kind of fast, isn't it? Did they hire your replacement already?"

"A slick hotshot from Chicago. I know I've been a little casual, but —"

"Cas, are you trying to tell me something?"

"You'll be okay. Keep your mouth shut and write like hell." He was worried about me. Casper never used profanity. He got up, patted my shoulder. "You might try . . . heels."

"Sure, Cas. Good idea." I shook his hand.

"There's a get-together tonight at Digger's and I invited the new supervisor. I thought it would be nice for her to meet the teams informally. Cocktails on Friday, business on Monday, like those soft lead-ins you like to write."

"Okay. See you then."

He'd done his best. It wasn't his fault I didn't fit. There was always the women's rack. Frilly blouses over a white bra, not gray thermal. But I needed the long underwear. There was too much I had to protect, too much at stake. As for drinks with the team at an upscale bar, I would rather have spent an hour locked in a rewrite session while Dylan screamed, "Limited-time offer!"

I worked late even though it was Friday, and I was late getting to Digger's. Casper pulled out a chair for me. I smiled hello to Mack and Nancy, the artists. One of the other creative team's members were clustered together and a couple of bigwigs from upstairs sat at the end of the table. Dylan was at the bar, flirting with the female bartender, a leggy number in a miniskirt.

Digger's catered to a professional crowd. There was a lot of greenery, smoking only in the balcony, and a juice bar adjoining the wet bar. It drew the folks who finished their day at the athletic club next door, exercise-conscious singles who weren't ready, even after a sauna, for a frozen dinner.

"What'll it be, Andy?"

Casper was drinking tonic and I ordered the same. Mack and Nancy were having wine. At the table's end, the big people were drinking whiskey. There was something about the way they held their bourbon, as though the glasses were heavy, but no more so than the day's weighty decisions. I filed the impression. Mack would know what I meant. He'd draw it. I caught his eye and he nodded. He rarely acknowledged me, and I sipped tonic to cover my smile.

Dylan came back from the bar and demanded a toast. "To Casper, the friendliest ghost I know."

I clinked glasses. "It'll be nice to have a friend upstairs."

Casper beamed but the bigwigs looked unsettled. Too much fraternizing between the artists and management, I supposed. I found Dylan's toast appropriate. Casper was too decent to get along in a business full of greedy goblins. I wondered if optimism and tonic would be enough to keep him meshed with the whiskey set.

I had my nose in my bubbles when Casper said, "Everyone, I'd like you to meet Gwen Severence. Ms. Severence," he said proudly, "these are the brightest people in the advertising business." He introduced us, beginning with Mack and ending with me.

Because I was on the end, I got up and gave her my chair, borrowing another from the next table. She was a tall woman, with long legs and a long waist, which meant she could look down on me whether she was standing or sitting. I hadn't pulled my hair back that morning and the scraggly ends curled on my shoulders. I pushed it behind my ears. Hers was short, darker than mine, almost jet, with bangs that framed her widely spaced eyes. I realized I was staring. Everyone was staring. She was stunning.

I said, "Gwen Severence."

She looked at me. "Yes?"

I felt myself blushing. I hadn't meant to say it out loud. "I was, um, trying to remember your name."

"And you're Andrea Stern."

"Right." I forgot to remind her that everyone at work called me Andy.

"Nice to meet you." She turned her attention to Mack and scarcely looked at me again.

She'd joined the wine drinkers. Her fingers twined the goblet stem but the glass never left the table. She sipped water and listened to the conversation. It was a neat trick. Either she wasn't a drinker or she chose not to drink with us, but she'd ordered wine to avoid the conjecture that non-drinkers inevitably faced. Cas and I had tonic, but we were square. No one expected us to imbibe.

I amused myself by staring at her profile. Her long nose was slightly hooked, a little less attractive from the side. I made the bird-of-prey comparison and began to fantasize. In adolescence, she'd dreamed of becoming a model but had to give it up. The camera caught the imperfections that made her interesting in person but unsuited for a magazine cover. She looked Italian and I wondered if she had brothers and sisters. She seemed remote; it was hard to picture her in a sibling pack. The wide eyes suggested a Greek heritage. Perhaps her grandparents had been peasants, her parents poor immigrants. I imagined that her mother had died young, leaving her to look after a taciturn father. That sort of difficult, romantic upbringing suited her appearance — driven yet reserved. I guessed that most people found her cold.

I hadn't meant to start thinking about Ryan. Ryan, who was muscular where this woman was slender, open in a way that made Gwen Severence seem tightly closed.

A voice very close to my ear whispered, "You're crying."

Startled, I looked into Gwen's eyes. For an instant, I saw concern, then cool curiosity. I was vaguely aware of dishes being passed, the aroma of chili sauce. Someone had ordered buffalo wings and another round.

"Excuse me." I used the commotion of food and drink to cover my exit.

Outside, the frigid air burned the tears from my

eyes. Ryan would be dead two years in spring. Why had I thought I could handle the social scene?

Gwen's voice asked, "Are you okay?"

I whirled, dismayed to see her. "I'm fine." She was shivering. Her leather jacket was top quality but too thin for February. She looked up and down the street. I asked, "Can I help you find something?"

"The subway or a taxi stand. I took a cab over because I was late."

"That way." I pointed. She was on heels. Not a subway commuter by a long shot. She'd be frozen by the time she got there. I zipped my parka. As she was turning away, I called, "Hey." She glanced back. "My car's around the corner. I'll give you a lift."

We fell into step and she said, "I'm totally lost in this town."

"You should get a hat and coat."

She seemed amused by my admonishment. "My luggage was delayed and I can't get a car from the dealer until tomorrow. I appreciate the ride."

Inside my economy model, I turned the heater on full blast. She gave me her address and I found it after a few tries. A nicer neighborhood than mine.

"Thanks, Andrea. Do you mind if I ask you something?"

"Sure."

"Why were you crying?"

"You reminded me of someone. The thought just came into my head."

"A woman?" When I nodded, she asked, "Do I look like her?"

"No. You're nothing alike."

"When did she dump you?"

I kept one hand on the steering wheel and wiped

my eyes with the other. "I'm gay, if that's what you want to know. It doesn't interfere with my work."

"I haven't reviewed your work yet. But if you want to survive in this business, you'd better toughen up."

Before she got out of the car, I said, "Go to hell."

"That's the idea." She slammed the car door.

On Monday morning at seven-thirty, my phone rang. "Andrea, it's Gwen."

"Oh. Hi." I had a listed number, just in case Mom decided to call about Julia.

Gwen said, "My car isn't ready, even though the dealer promised. If I start calling for rentals, I'll be late. Can you find your way back here?"

"Give me fifteen minutes." When I arrived she was standing outside, still in her leather jacket. "No luggage yet, huh?"

"This move's been a bitch."

I turned on public radio and drove us to work.

She turned the volume down. "I studied the portfolios this weekend."

"Oh, yeah?" I concentrated on traffic.

"What's your opinion of the material your team puts out?"

"Mack and Nancy are great artists," I said without hesitation. "Dylan is trite and Casper makes everything look like an ad."

"Why shouldn't an ad look like an ad?"

Traffic was heavy. I changed lanes. "Who did you work for in Chicago?"

"Branagan and Company."

"What position?"

"Creative director."

"You were in charge of creative for a firm that big?"

"Yeah. What do you think an ad should look like?"

I shrugged. "Normal. I don't like aggressive visuals. Concepts should look and sound natural. I think our stuff is cluttered. And no one listens to trite copy. I don't care how many times you say it." I glanced at her. "How come you're dumbing down?"

She laughed. "I thought you said you weren't aggressive."

"You're overqualified for Casper's job."

"I'm out of practice. I was out of work for a year."

Traffic was crawling and I studied her profile. In the dim light of the bar, her eyes had looked bruised. Now I could see why I'd had that impression. The irises were very dark, the skin beneath her lower lids so pale that the bluish veins showed. Her cheeks were neither creamy nor ruddy, just pale. Another woman might have worn too much rouge, or paid for a tanning booth. I imagined that if Gwen got outdoors in the summer, she would tan nicely. But she had the sunless skin of an office mole.

A merging car drew my attention to the road, then I glanced back at Gwen. When taken individually — the longish nose, high forehead curtained by dark bangs — her features weren't exceptional. She didn't glamorize with makeup, wearing just enough to accent lips and eyes. But the overall effect claimed my gaze again and again. She met my eyes. Quickly, I stared out the windshield. It was her eyes. They were huge, forceful in their desire. Sexy. The expression was the focal point of her appearance.

Curious, I asked, "Is your family Greek?"

"Italian."

She should eat more pasta, I thought. She was thin.

I exited the snarled expressway. The only advantage to working in the suburban outskirts was not having to pay a garage fee. The neighborhood was full of dentists' offices and drive-through coffee shops.

"How come you came to Boston? Why not New York?"

"This is a good place for me right now. The right size agency." As I was parking, she said, "About your portfolio. You're holding back."

"Did Casper tell you that?"

"No, but if he can see it then he's smarter than I gave him credit for. I only work with people who give me total quality."

"Careful. You're starting to sound like Dylan. A little trite."

"Dylan and I spoke by phone on Saturday. We reached an agreement on his severance package." I pulled my key out of the ignition. Gwen tucked her hands into her pockets. Without the heater running, the car was instantly cold. She said, "Your résumé is lean. You wrote for a specialty magazine for a year. Before that, just filler. I've seen college interns with more experience. People like Casper give to charity. I don't. The only reason you didn't get a Saturday-morning phone call is because some of the clients like your work. Not the stuff Dylan wrote over. But Casper let some of your copy stand."

"I didn't submit everything for approval."

"Don't pull a stunt like that with me. And if you want to keep your merit raise, don't miss a deadline."

"I've never missed a deadline."

"That was when Casper managed the workload. Not me."

"Did Casper tell you that I hate teamwork and my attitude sucks?"

"If you have time for attitude, you're not busy enough. I'll take care of that."

"May I ask a question?"

She shivered. "I'll indulge you because you gave me a ride. But hurry up. Your car is freezing."

"Who dumped you? Girlfriend? Boyfriend? A few of each? Heartache or heartburn — what's making you so bitchy? If you'd told me sooner, I could have stopped at the drugstore for Midol."

She chuckled. "Save your quips for your copy. And Andrea." She waited until I met her eyes. "I expect you to get it right every time, not just when you feel like it." As she climbed out, she said, "Don't be late. It's your first day with the new boss and you already know I'm not nice."

As I watched her cross the parking lot, my inner voice sassed, *She caught you.*

I climbed slowly out of my car. The temperature was below freezing but I didn't hurry inside. I recalled Casper's pat wisdom: "Words are not flesh and blood." I had a mental image of Gwen, steak knife in hand, testing the meatiness of my copy.

141

I'd hoped for more time, a longer grace period. In a panic, I wondered if I was good enough. Could I write a successful piece, not by stealing someone else's tone but using my own? I remembered the college essay in which I'd first set down my own thoughts, the one that had earned me a B plus instead of an A. I recalled my writing notebooks. I'd been so hopeful. Then Ryan had died and I'd given up. I remembered the fever-dream, the glow that her touch had drawn from my chest.

It's in here.

"Idiot," I snarled. How wrong I'd been. I didn't have her heart. My own pathetic organ beat in my chest, puny and flailing. I'd buried myself under goosedown and I was as lukewarm as ever.

Stay hot, she'd said. And I remembered, finally, why she'd loved me. *"When you study, you get hot."*

I had my parka off before I got inside. "Okay," I muttered.

When I got to my desk, I balked. Files were stacked on either side of my computer. The office manager came in and covered up what was left of my in-basket.

"Sorry, Andy. I was told to give you everything that Dylan was working on, plus some extras." She looked grim. "Wait till you see your e-mail. The new boss likes to work at home."

I rolled up my sleeves. I was already sweating. Impatiently, I pulled off my blouse and went to work in my long-sleeved gray undershirt. Every once in a while I muttered, "Okay," and kept my head bent over my desk.

Chapter 11

Within a week, the office was in an uproar. Dylan wasn't the only one to get walking papers. Casper's teams were decimated, then consolidated under Gwen's supervision. Mack and Nancy gave notice and announced the opening of their own graphic arts business. Why work twice as hard for Gwen when they could do it for themselves? Her bitchiness didn't really bother me. I was just as rude right back, and we seemed to get along better for our mutual ill-temper. She wasn't patronizing as Casper had been; when I sniped at her, she gave me more work to do.

At the end of the second week, she was at my desk holding a folder of copy I'd submitted. It was after five on Friday. I glanced around but my co-workers had beat it. They were on their way home or to the bar for stiff drinks. My vote was with the drinkers.

"What's left," she asked, "when you make a sundae without ice cream, without fudge and missing the cherry?"

"I give up. A frozen yogurt account?"

"Marshmallow fluff." She slid the folder across my desk.

I tossed it back into my in-basket. "I'm working my ass off for you."

"Your ass isn't worth the cheap furniture you're sitting on." My blouse was draped over the back of my chair. I was working in my thermal shirt again. Her eyes glinted. "You'll catch pneumonia."

"I already had it. What's it to you, anyway?"

"Why do you work so hard if you hate it?"

Her question caught me off guard. "I don't hate —" I broke off. "I don't know if I'm good enough." After a minute, I added, "I want to be."

She turned to leave. "Have a nice weekend. You can fix that crap on Monday."

The following week, I tried again. The old feeling was there — the nuance. I had a sense for what the clients wanted. It was my old trick, the way I used to write for teachers, but it wasn't good enough for Gwen. I was beside myself trying to figure it out — how to please the client, how to satisfy her. I was coming in early, staying late and sweating my way through all my clean shirts. And it wasn't working. I submitted a few pieces. One came back with the

144

word, "Fluff," scrawled over the top. Another one just said, "No."

Gwen spent a lot of time upstairs. In spite of that, she had no trouble keeping our desks full. It seemed to me that she was doing Casper's job and then some. The rest of us kept our pencils sharp and our computer screens glowing. When she wasn't around, Gwen was called bitch and super-bitch. The anger was normal. She acted like she owned us. But I also sensed respect. Barbarian people skills aside, she knew what she was doing in advertising.

The rumors were relentless.

"AIDS," someone said.

"I heard it was the big C."

"With that gorgeous hair? Chemo would be a crime."

"Heart attack." It was the most persistent theory, the one that stuck.

Someone heard it from a cousin in Chicago who had a boyfriend in the ad business, or some other ridiculous route. Gwen had been on the rise, then she was gone. Vanished. A year later here she was in Boston, crunching our backbones like gravel while she climbed toward a corner office.

Discontent was an undercurrent, but excitement began to swell. We weren't being held to a higher standard for nothing. Our product was getting better. Under Casper, as I had complained, ads were unremarkable, one sometimes indistinguishable from the next. With Gwen in charge, original concepts began to stand out. I recognized it immediately as her unique style and studied it.

By mid-March, I was exhausted. Over the weekend, I did laundry but stopped short of ironing blouses. There was no food in my apartment. Like the rest of the office, I'd been living on take-out. I glanced in the mirror. My reflection was sallow, but from fatigue, not malnutrition. I looked in my checkbook. Not great, not bad. I was paying back Mom. It was time to write to Julia, so I dug out a notecard and penned a few lines about work and, to my surprise, about Gwen. On impulse, I addressed it to Mom as well. Since I was driving to work on her dime, I guessed she had a right to hear the news.

In the afternoon, propelled by restlessness and the weak sunshine, I went shopping. I circled the mall and stopped at the sporting goods store; when I came out, I had a bag full of rugby shirts. The smell of roasting coffee lured me into a gourmet boutique, where I purchased a desk-sized coffeemaker and ground beans. Satisfied with my errands, I went home and slept for the rest of the weekend.

On Monday I got in early, dressed in jeans, boots and a rugby shirt. I set up the coffeepot, got it brewing and turned on my computer. It was seven-fifteen. I headed outside, hatless, gloveless, wearing only a down vest. I'd packed away the parka with the blouses. On the street, I went in search of something other than a convenience market, something more appealing than cellophane doughnuts. A few blocks up, I found an Italian bakery and bought butter cookies — plain, with jelly, sprinkled with seeds, and fancy ones with pine nuts. I was settling in to work when Gwen came in.

"God, that smells good." She was holding a coffee cup from the mini-mart.

I said, "Ditch that," and poured her a mug.

I figured she'd take it to her own office, but she sat down and watched me open files. I passed her the bakery box.

She took a seeded cookie. "I haven't had these in ages. My mother used to make them."

"According to office gossip, you were spawned by an evil computer program. You're an animated arch-villain come to life. Brilliant, but inhuman." She laughed and nibbled her cookie. Her lips were nice, full, not too much lipstick. I looked away. "The stuff you do is great."

"What have you got to show me?"

I said miserably, "Nothing fits. Your style, what the clients think they want — it's two different things. I'm not Casper. I can't paste it together."

"That's good news."

I was almost pleading. "What do you want?"

She stood up, brushed the crumbs from her skirt. "Andrea, I want you to write for me."

I sipped coffee while my screen-saver flashed. Around me, my co-workers began arriving.

Someone said, "Who's the hick?"

I realized they meant me.

I got a pat on the back. "You could have just asked her to fire you."

I was taking a ribbing for dressing down. Gwen had sat with me and hadn't said anything. I went back to staring at my screen-saver.

Write for me.

I could forget about selling to clients or relying on marketing data. Casper used to bring down the demographics like he was delivering stone tablets.

Write for me.

From now on there was one person I had to reach. Whatever I wanted the public to feel, she had to feel it first. My writing had to touch her.

I kept the folders closed. I already knew the product information. I outlined a few ideas, then wrote steadily through lunch. I stuck to the same schedule all week and wore jeans every day. By the time Gwen came in at seven-thirty, I had coffee on and Italian cookies. Late in the afternoon on Friday, she was at my shoulder. Wordlessly, I passed her a few pages.

She said, "Nice." I didn't look up, but I could tell she meant it. She gave me a file. "I stole this client from Chicago. The copy deadline's Monday but I'd like to get the artwork started tonight. Can you stay late?"

"Sure."

She helped herself to stale cookies on her way out.

The client was a travel company selling middle-class cruise packages and excursions for upper-crust patrons. Destinations ranged from Mexico to Alaska. They wanted one campaign theme. In my mind there was only one customer. I pictured Gwen boarding a ship. As it got underway, she was alone on deck. The ship never docked; she didn't disembark. She lay on a sun-drenched chaise and danced by herself in starlight. As she strode through the dining room, the captain, the only other soul in sight, bowed. Her fingers brushed an ice-sculpture. She left the sumptuous banquet untouched.

All around her the ocean and sky were a singular

blue, the ship a golden vessel. Against this backdrop she wore gauzy, nearly see-through white. I wrote an aerial scene — water, boat, woman — blue, gold, white. I'd pushed my keyboard aside and was scribbling furiously on a notepad. I wished Mack hadn't quit. I wondered who Gwen would get to do the art. Finally, I penciled in the caption, the theme to bring it together. *We made this voyage for you.*

I stretched and heard my back pop, then glanced at my watch. Five-forty. I had an hour's worth of typing before I could show her a reasonable draft. I grabbed the keyboard. While the draft was printing, I flipped through the restaurant menus in my desk. There was a Chinese place that wasn't too greasy. Better still, they delivered. I had the phone in my hand. What would I eat, I wondered, if I'd had a heart attack? I ordered vegetarian mu shu, curried shrimp, steamed vegetables and brown rice. Security called me when the food came and I carried the warm bags and my finished copy into Gwen's office. Everyone else had gone home. I wondered again who was going to do the art.

I handed her the folder. Sauce was leaking through a bag so I retreated hastily for paper towels. When I came back, she had a sketchpad in her lap. I let the food sit and watched quietly. When she turned the sketch I saw my boat — gold on a sea of blue. It was a pencil drawing but my mind easily filled in the colors. And on the deck, just as I'd pictured it, a woman in a sheer gown. It billowed, then clung to her body. I could see the movement.

I nodded. "That's it exactly."

She blocked in the motto and tore off the page. "I'll fax this with your copy now and finish the sketches tomorrow. We'll set up production next week."

"Does Casper get a look?"

She hesitated. "I report to the partners." She strode off to send her fax.

I sat, stunned. No wonder she spent so much time upstairs. If it was true, and I didn't doubt her, then what was Casper doing? My growling stomach reminded me that I'd skipped lunch. I set out the cartons, chopsticks, cups of green tea.

When Gwen came back, she said, "Is that Chinese? Thank God, I'm starved." She reached for her pocketbook. "What do I owe you?"

"Nothing. Um, I forgot to get plates."

"Do you mind sharing? I'm not contagious." I looked up quickly, then tried to cover my embarrassment by fussing with my chopsticks. Gwen said, "I can't remember eating anything today except Italian cookies. I guess that's two meals I owe you for."

"My treat." I handed her the shrimp.

She took a bite and sighed. "That's wonderful."

I dug into the mu shu. After a while, we traded.

I said, "I didn't know you were an artist."

"That's how I got started." She smiled. "It was fun tonight. Maybe I'll do the art for all your copy."

"I wouldn't mind."

"It's great when you get it right. There's no feeling like it."

"I'm no expert."

She contemplated me. "How come you went into advertising?"

"I needed a job."

"Was your girlfriend in the business? The one who dumped you?"

I swallowed. "No. And she didn't dump me, exactly. She died."

Gwen stopped eating. "I'm sorry."

"It was a couple of years ago."

She swiveled her chair and stared out the window. "How did it happen?"

"Heart failure."

"Drugs?"

"It's called cardiomyopathy. Her heart muscle was diseased but it was undiagnosed, probably congenital." Gwen was silent, still facing the window. I asked, "What about you? Everyone thinks you had a heart attack."

"I contracted an amoebic infection in South America. The dysentery was ghastly and then the little buggers did the backstroke all the way to my heart. One moment I was chatting, the next thing I knew, I was dead. Someone called an ambulance and the doctors got my heart started." My own heart was thumping. "At least, that's what I was told. I remember a slightly different version of events." She faced me. "After something like that, people treat you differently. When I could work again, I wanted a new environment."

"I keep to myself," I said.

We sat quietly. Finally, Gwen said, "There's something you don't know about yourself. You're the original soft-sell. Everyone says it doesn't work. The gurus don't recommend it. But it comes naturally to you. It reads like a dream when you get it right."

"I wrote the piece that way on purpose. You're romantic, almost tragic. I just wrote what I knew you'd like." I rummaged through a bag and tossed her a fortune cookie.

"I think this ad had a little of you in it." She handed back the cookie. "I don't eat those anymore. I was in a Chinese restaurant when I had my heart attack."

"In South America?" No wonder it almost killed her.

"On the way home, I stopped in San Francisco to visit my brother. I was over the dysentery by then but I'd lost so much weight he decided to treat me to dinner. It was one of those fancy places — Peking duck, chrysanthemums in the soup."

I looked at the congealing mu shu and felt like an idiot. There was no way I could impress her. Until this moment, I hadn't realized how hard I'd been trying.

Gwen said, "I opened my cookie and fell out of my chair."

"What did it say?"

"Some nonsense about health and happiness."

I threw the unopened cookies into the trash and cleared the mess off her desk. I gave her half of the leftovers.

She said, "See you tomorrow?"

"Yeah."

I was almost home before I remembered that

tomorrow was Saturday. I took a shower and fell into bed. Why not work six days a week? I was beginning to enjoy it.

Gwen did more of the art for my copy. She was better than Mack, or maybe I was giving her better stuff to work with. When we collaborated, we sniped at each other less often.

She said, "Your ideas are easy to draw. You're very visual."

I glowed from her praise. I was also giddy from the creative freedom. Previously, concepts had been dictated by the director, arriving piecemeal on my desk after Casper had divvied up the team assignments. Often Mack and Nancy had done the art first, leaving me to fill in the blanks with words of the right length. By the time the designs were hacked apart and put back together, the ads looked like lunchmeat. Gwen gave me whole concepts to work with and I loved her for it.

One rainy morning, I brought her a cup of coffee with my latest copy.

"Andrea, do me a favor? Pamper me in private, or at least after hours."

I flushed hotly and scurried back to my desk. Before, I'd been the team oddball. Now I was the boss's pet. I wore jeans and got away with it. Because I came in early and stayed late, I was accused of ass-kissing. Conversations at the water cooler stifled as I approached.

For my part, I viewed my hostile co-workers as irritating siblings. I treasured the quiet early hours when I was in the office alone, or with Gwen, and worked impatiently through the afternoon, waiting for the grumblers to go home. On some mornings Gwen brought in freshly ground beans. I kept the coffee brewing, hoping to see her. When we worked late, or on Saturdays, we took turns ordering out.

My anger, the attitude that Casper had complained about, had abated. What I felt was more like radio static, the noise between stations. Gwen was all static on the surface, too, but when we worked together we both got quiet.

One morning as I was pouring coffee, some of the hot liquid splashed from the carafe, staining the white stripe on my favorite shirt.

"Damn." I stuck the material in my mouth, sucking to get the stain out.

Gwen walked in. "What are you doing?"

I said, "It's true. This stuff is good to the last drop."

She laughed and whacked me softly on the head with the file she was holding. "I'll take some in a mug if you don't mind." I poured carefully. "Thanks, Andrea." She touched a finger to the spot on my chest. "Put some cold water on that."

I stared dumbly after her, then shut off the coffeemaker and carried the empty carafe to the bathroom. I rinsed the pot and dabbed at the stain. The coffee spot stuck stubbornly to my shirt.

I said, "Shit," but my heart wasn't in the complaint.

I faced myself in the full-length mirror. As usual, my hair needed a trim. But I looked more substantial in jeans and boots. I caught myself smiling and turned quickly away. I grabbed the coffeepot and went back to my desk.

It was useless to wonder if Gwen liked me. She drank my coffee and took my copy. She gave me hell if my writing was bad, moderate praise when she liked a particular turn of phrase. And sometimes, in moments that I looked forward to, she expressed genuine pleasure. I worked for that, to please her. She was like an envelope, a place where I could stuff some of my burdensome pain. Never mind that it tore open by the time I got home. Each day I shoved a little more hurt out of sight.

Chapter 12

It was another Saturday, a rainy April morning, and I was working contentedly, oblivious to the weather or the weekend. Gwen came in wearing straight-leg jeans and a pocket T-shirt. She usually dressed up, even on Saturday.

"Hi, Gwen." She looked thin but maybe it was the jeans. "Did you skip breakfast? I'll get us something at the bakery." I reached for my windbreaker.

She shuddered. "I don't feel like eating." She picked up the hard copy from my printer tray.

"Don't read that."

"Is this the wine? It's too long. We're doing a thirty-second spot."

"I know. I'm working on something. Give it back."

She held onto it. "You've got two minutes' worth of material. Where are you going with this?"

"I want to educate the consumer."

She sat down. "Go on."

"Wine is intimidating. People read the labels and guess. No one really knows how to pick a good wine."

"Red with meat, white with fish?"

"Venison with Cabernet. Chenin Blanc and Dover sole."

She looked pasty. "Stop talking about food. What about the wine?"

I had an image of Gwen in a wine cellar, her body taut as she reached for a bottle. Her clothes were burgundy-colored, the bottles like glowing jewels. On an oak cask, two glasses stood ready. She made her selection and caressed the label. The caption wrote itself in my mind. *Know what you're tasting.*

I blinked. "I want to do a series, like a televised wine-tasting. In each segment the consumer learns about bouquet, or tannin, the different types of grapes." On my desk I had a book on domestic vineyards and an oenophile's dictionary. "The wine keeps its mystique but the consumer feels cultured."

"Okay, Bacchus. I'll pitch it." She stood up and swayed slightly.

"Are you okay?"

"I'm fine." She handed back my copy.

"You should eat."

"No food."

"Well, put a sweater on or something."

She snapped, "Cut the Jewish grandmother crap."

"Do you mind if I keep you alive until my next raise?"

She put a hand to her head. "I need some aspirin."

Not on an empty stomach. I bit my tongue. I said matter-of-factly, "Go home."

She turned to leave, swayed again and sat down quickly. "Shit. I feel sick."

I said more gently, "I'll drive you."

"I can drive."

I helped her up. "I'll follow and make sure you get there. If you get dizzy you can pull over."

"Do you always fuss so much?"

"Jewish grandmother genes."

She drove to her building and parked in a private garage. I circled the block but couldn't find parking. Finally, I stopped at a market and lugged a bag of groceries back up the street. In the foyer, I was met by a doorman.

"I'm delivering these for Gwen Severence."

He picked up a phone, dialed, hung up. "She's not in. Leave them here."

"Please try again. I saw her drive in." I had visions of Gwen passed out in her car. "My name's Andrea," I added. "I'm a friend." He announced me and nodded to the elevators. "Can you tell me the number?" He looked suspicious, so I said, "She's sick. I'm bringing groceries."

"Three-oh-four."

The building was only three stories, a renovated Gothic structure. On the third floor, I peered up and down the hall and spotted a door slightly ajar.

"Gwen?" When she didn't answer, I nosed in and spied her leather jacket. I pushed inside. "Gwen?"

The ceilings were impossibly high, and my first thought was how much it would cost to heat. The living area was messy — modern furniture strewn with the morning's paper. A coffee mug, minus a coaster, sat on the glass table. I could see the kitchen and partway down a hall. From that direction came sounds like retching. Poor Gwen. What was she doing getting the flu in April? The rest of the office had been sick in February, except for me. I'd had pneumonia in January.

In the kitchen I unpacked bottled seltzer, lime soda, canned broth and aspirin. I looked in the freezer for ice and found a stack of frozen dinners. I grimaced.

"Andrea?" Gwen was in a bathrobe, her face pale, the ends of her hair damp. "What are you doing here?"

"I brought you fluids."

For some reason, standing in Gwen's kitchen made me think of my mother. I remembered her fighting with Dad, planning tournament strategies with Julia. I remembered her exasperation when I refused to grow up and get feminine. She'd been determined, disapproving, except when I was sick. Then she sat beside me and placed damp towels on my forehead as I lay in bed. She held my hand while waiting for the thermometer to register, then gave me sips of soda through a long straw.

I mumbled, "I forgot the straws."

"What?" Gwen said distractedly, "If you want something, help yourself. I need to lie down."

"Here." I poured a glass of warm soda and handed her two aspirin. "Call if you need anything else." I made sure the door locked behind me.

I bought another bag of groceries on the way home, then got busy in my kitchen. While a chicken was roasting, I chopped onions and celery for soup. I chose mild seasonings — sage and fresh parsley for vitamin C. When the chicken was cool I shredded the meat, boiled the bones and strained the broth. I ladled in the ingredients, covered the pot and let it simmer. Gwen wouldn't be able to eat for a few days, but when she opened her freezer I wanted her to find home cooking.

By the time I was done bustling it was evening, Saturday night. I flopped onto the couch, turned on the TV and quickly turned it off. Briefly, I considered going back to work. At the office, I'd think about Gwen. At home, cooking chicken, I was thinking about Ryan. Without meaning to, I fell asleep.

In my dream I saw Ryan. She was far away and her arm rotated through the air like a windmill, beckoning. *Come here.* I walked toward her and stopped, looked down. I was at the ocean's edge, waves lapping over my feet. Ryan was still far off, standing in the water. I craned my neck, shaded my eyes. She waved me forward.

I called, "I can't. Come to me." I thought, *She must be on a raft.* Just then a swell lifted her and I saw that her legs ended at the knees, feet submerged. "Oh, Ryan," I whispered. "What are you trying to do?" Was she rising up or sinking? I couldn't tell.

She kept waving, and I could see that she was looking past me. I turned, and there was Gwen. She waved to Ryan and walked into the ocean.

160

"Fools," I yelled. "You'll drown." But Gwen was crossing on the surface. When she was beyond the breaker line, she began to sink. As she dropped lower, so did Ryan. "I knew it," I screamed. "It's impossible."

Ryan's face looked peaceful; I couldn't see Gwen's expression. Soon they were up to their necks. One head went under, then the other.

They'll come up. They're playing a trick on me.

Waves broke at my feet. The ocean's surface remained empty.

I woke up clammy with sweat. I roused myself from the couch, stripped and showered. In my bedroom, I crawled under the covers and stared into the darkness. What the hell did Gwen think she was doing going after Ryan like that?

To reassure myself, I said aloud, "It was a dream."

Lying in bed, I remembered my childhood swimming lessons. Kids clung like leeches along the side of the pool. The bigger ones, Julia included, curled their toes over the pool's lip, hooked their arms around their ears and dove in. I sat on the steps, the shallow water lapping my belly, hugged my knees and tried not to shiver. The first summer, I didn't swim at all. But the next year, maybe because the sun was hotter, or because I'd grown tired of the steps, I put my face in and learned to swim. Julia, arms churning like mixing-bowl beaters, legs frog-kicking, breast-stroked the length of the pool. Doggedly, I paddled after her.

I dozed. I saw Ryan and Gwen, heads bobbing, and Julia, my sister.

I can't get to them. They're too deep.

I hated them for going too far, for being out of reach. More than anything, I hated being left behind.

In the morning, I loaded my car with groceries and the Sunday paper. The soup, in a freezer container, sat on my passenger seat. At Gwen's, I double-parked and the doorman scowled when I left the bags by the elevator.

"Please call Gwen Severence. I'll take her groceries up as soon as I find parking." When I got back, I repeated, "Call her."

He grunted into the phone and gave me the go-ahead. "You woke her up."

I shuttled everything to Gwen's door, caught my breath and knocked.

She was still in her bathrobe, still pale. "Andrea?"

"I made you soup."

She groaned. "I can't eat."

"You have to sip clear liquids and take aspirin to keep the fever down." I carried the groceries into the kitchen. She didn't argue when I said, "Go back to bed." I put eggs, bread and oranges into her refrigerator, tea and honey in the cupboard. The soup went into the freezer.

I brought her a fresh glass of soda. "Take tiny sips." I'd remembered to get straws.

She wet her lips. "Why are you doing this?"

"You'd probably rather be alone." She nodded. "You wouldn't drink enough fluids. Eventually, you'd schlep to the store for orange juice. You wouldn't think of eating soup and you'd get better anyway."

"God, Andrea. Go away."

I had a few more instructions. "When you can manage it, try warm broth and dry toast. And don't come to work." I implored my Jewish ancestors, *I tried.*

As I was leaving, I remembered the paper and carried it back to the bedroom. Gwen was curled on her side, eyes closed. I lay the Sunday *Globe* at the foot of her bed. The room had nice colors — very pale greens and pinks. Subtle shades. Anyone else could easily have overdone it, like an Easter basket. But she'd kept the tones muted. With the windows open and a breeze coming in, it would feel like a garden. It was the kind of effect that people craved all winter. Gwen had planned for it, knowing as she decorated in February how welcome it would be come April. She stirred under the covers. I showed myself out.

She was out of work for a few days. In our section of the agency, people began working normal nine-to-five hours and taking long lunches. They loafed beside one another's desks and made frequent trips to the mini-mart. My workload, without Gwen's constant input, was also lighter.

On Wednesday night she called me at home. "Am I interrupting anything?"

I clicked off the news. "Nope. How're you feeling?"

"Better. Still weak," she admitted. "It's taking forever to get over this."

"Do you need anything? I'll go to the market."

"I've never had so much food in my refrigerator." She paused. "Thanks for the soup."

"Sure."

"I really appreciated the Sunday paper."

"Uh-huh."

"If you don't mind my asking, what do you do in your free time?"

"Florence Nightingale impersonations." She laughed but sounded tired. "I work for a workaholic," I said. "I don't have free time."

"Can you get off early tomorrow and bring some stuff over? I wouldn't ask, except —"

"It's too soon for you to come back," I insisted. "What do you want?"

"Bring all the client folders in my in-basket. And my sketchpad."

On Thursday evening, the doorman on duty recognized me. When I got off the elevator, Gwen's door was ajar and I slipped inside. Her color was better and her eyes were clear. She was wearing jeans and a sloppy sweater and still looked thin. I gave her the files.

"There's soda in the fridge." She smiled. "Help yourself." I made two mugs of honey-sweetened tea while she spread everything on the coffee table. "My laptop's in the bedroom. Do you mind?"

Her sheets had been changed. That effort alone must have exhausted her. The computer was on the nightstand. Grimly, I picked it up, and the notes beside it. Had I known she'd been working in bed, I wouldn't have brought her the files so readily.

Who was I kidding? I'd do whatever she asked. I needed Gwen — the attention she gave me, the praise, even her criticism. Under Casper, I'd written with the surface part of my brain and kept my feelings as deeply buried as Ryan's casket. With Gwen, emotion was seeping back. Where I'd flattened myself, curves and angles were taking shape. It was like having an adolescent body again, and I was uncomfortable. I knew that Gwen was responsible, at least in part, for my resurgence. I had no idea if she knew of her effect on me.

I carried her notes and the laptop into the living room.

Ignoring my frown, she logged on. After a while, she said, "Stop hovering."

She hadn't asked me to leave, so I went into the kitchen. I rinsed the bowls that had gathered in the sink and loaded them into the dishwasher, then bagged the trash and put a clean liner in the can. Having made myself scarce for five minutes, I went back to the living room.

Gwen was bent over the computer. Every few minutes she used her fingers to scrape back her bangs. Long bangs, long fingers. Everything about her was lean. In spite of her thinness, she wasn't frail. Having made that observation, I felt somewhat relieved.

She didn't look up. "What's happening at the office?"

"Not much."

"Not much has changed or not much is happening because no one's working?"

"The latter."

"What about you?"

"I could use your input." I sorted through the files and handed her the copy I'd been working on.

She set it aside, then divided everything else into piles. "Rubber bands are in the kitchen drawer." I brought her a handful and she gave me one set of banded files after another. "Give these to Jeff and these to Donna."

"They're not gonna take directions from me."

"I've already e-mailed everyone their assignments. They're to fax me updates on projects by noon tomorrow."

"You have a fax machine here?"

She pointed to the telephone stand. "I'll do the art for your copy tonight. Can you pick it up in the morning?"

"Sure."

"If it's a hassle, I'll messenger it."

"I'll come over."

She sat back. "You've been a big help, Andrea. You've made this easier."

"You're welcome."

"I want to ask you something. What's your motivation?"

Her question danced before me like a cobra in front of a snake charmer. No matter which way I tried to duck, it would follow.

I shrugged, stalled. "What do you mean?"

"You're not the type to brown-nose. You do your work whether or not I'm looking over your shoulder. And because I like you, your peers don't."

I could give a damn about my peers. I said, "You treat people like they're expendable and they resent it. They're slacking this week, but most of the time they work hard for you."

She smiled. "Very noble. Jeff and Donna are still going to hate you tomorrow."

"I'll live." I began to sidle toward the door.

"Do you want to know why I was hired?"

I came to a halt. "You're starting fresh. You needed a new environment, less stress or something."

She waved a hand over the mess on the coffee table. "Does this look stress-free?"

"No."

"You'll have to keep it to yourself."

"You've won my loyalty. Don't bribe me with company secrets."

She seemed amused. "I can't bribe you unless I know what you want. The only thing I really know about you is that you hurt like hell. That's why your writing is such a surprise. You have a soft touch." She was staring at me. "I wonder what you were like before your lover died. You must have let some of the sweet stuff show."

"I was shy."

She returned her attention to the laptop. "I'll see you in the morning. Anyone with questions can e-mail me."

I could have kicked myself. Gwen was like a morning glory, a flower that opened for a brief part of the day and then shut tightly. I'd missed a chance to peek inside.

Why should I care?

It wasn't my business where she worked, or why. But I was cooking for her, and that was a sure sign that I cared too much.

She looked up again. I was standing indecisively between the sofa and her front door.

She asked, "Are you going or staying?"

I inched back to the sofa and sat down. "I don't gossip."

She tapped a few keys and logged off. "I was

offered a partnership, contingent on my increasing profits. I've already attracted new business and cut production costs."

"You mean the layoffs were your idea."

"I was on a partnership track before — Anyhow, our product has a new look and we can charge more for it." She crossed her arms. "Some people still aren't pulling their weight."

"Everyone knows you're good. But they can't sustain the level you're after."

"Casper and his damn teams. I want a stable of independent artists and writers. Let talent decide who gets the projects and the raises. Casper wants kindergarten."

"You think it's more mature for us to compete with one another?"

"You'd be surprised how well it works. You'll thrive on it."

"I don't think so."

"You hate teams."

"That doesn't mean I want to fight over scraps like dogs in a kennel."

She smiled. "No dogs. I'll leave that part out of the memo."

A nagging thought surfaced. "What's Casper doing?"

"Fighting with me, mostly. I'm winning."

"And if you get to be a partner? Then what?" I couldn't imagine her leaving Casper in charge. She already seemed to have most of the creative control. She didn't answer. After a moment, I said, "Shit. You're pushing him out."

"I didn't think you'd be upset about it."

"He hired me."

"And let you sit around like unexploded dynamite."

I was busy mulling. "Isn't three partners a little top heavy?"

"Bryant's retiring. Maybe as early as this summer. The news will be out soon enough." She searched my face. "I thought you'd be excited. Andrea, I can help you showcase your talent."

"Maybe I don't want a . . . showcase."

She shook her head. "Is there any way to make you happy?"

Do you care if I'm happy? Of course she didn't. I was only a means to an end, the words that underscored the art. But she was useful to me, too. When I gave her what she wanted, life was smoother. Strangers no longer seemed to be made of sandpaper, roughing me up as I brushed past. Around Gwen, I hurt less. And that was more valuable to me than my paycheck.

I could tell she was tired. I was weary, too. I said, "Do whatever you want. Dump Casper, concentrate on your own career. Teams, kindergarten, the dog kennel. I don't care. There's only one reason I go to work in the morning."

She met my eyes. "What's that?"

"You."

I saw something in the corner, a moving shadow. And then it was beside me, winking one great eye and threatening to drool on my knee. The fuzzy beast, the monster, my fear.

I hate you, I flung at him. *Every time I stand to lose someone, you come skulking around. Leave me alone.*

He grinned and nuzzled closer.

I stood up, leaned to Gwen and kissed the top of her head. She smelled like sweat and sleep, an at-home smell. "Goodnight. See you tomorrow."

She watched me go. I doubted that she saw the monster nipping my heels or heard his scratching claws. He was all mine, chuckling and slobbering, a devoted companion.

Chapter 13

At home I was afraid to turn on the lights, and afraid not to. When I did, I discovered that the beast hadn't followed me. He was out somewhere in the misty night, partying in an alley probably, celebrating the opportunity to torment me again.

And whose fault is that? my inner voice scorned.

Mine.

Try as I might to convince myself that I was only using Gwen, beast-breath wasn't coming after me for the ads. He sought the fuel, the emotion that drove me.

"No." I spoke to the window. "You can't have it. Not Casper and not you." I was giving it to Gwen, but only on paper. I was safe that way, I reasoned. "They're just ads," I said. But Gwen inspired me, and the fuzzy monster knew it.

Gwen knew, too, from my confession, if she hadn't already gleaned the obvious from my work. What motivated me? Money was a minor factor. A showcase? Artistic credit? It hardly mattered. Gwen was the important thing. Grief, for me, wasn't a shell, a thin casing to be cracked. It was a canyon gutting through me. Gwen forced me down and there, struggling up like sparse growth after a brush fire, I noticed silly things like curiosity, affection. Because I had nothing else to do with them, I directed the feelings at Gwen. There was a bigger feeling, too, that I'd unearthed. It was getting harder to ignore the fact that I was attracted to her.

Inadvertently, I glanced down. Not out the window but down inside. Without caution I began nosing around, like a kid kicking through an empty lot after a carnival. There was the usual trash — my confidence as flat as thready peanut husks, crunched into the tar. I saw sticky soda puddles, the used cups tossed by the breeze, bumping across the asphalt. That's how lightweight, how bruised I felt.

Deep down, I'd hoped for rock piles and smoldering, burned-out craters. I'd hoped that the debris of my love for Ryan would be visible like great, irradiated boulders, as dangerous as uranium ore, unapproachable, the pulsing glow forcing me to keep my distance. But I saw none of that. Just crumpled candy wrappers that reminded me of the ads I tried to write, and there weren't even very many of those.

Gone were the painful shards — horrifying yet beautiful; I would rather have had those vivid, frightening dimensions. Anything but this boring waste. Dismayed, I noticed a fissure, steam seeping up as though a hot spring lurked below. I ran over and got the toe of my boot in the crack, wedged my foot, then my leg inside. I could feel the heat and moisture. I dropped down.

Steam was blowing; I heard it hiss. The walls were rock, sweating and breathing. Heaving. I could see them breathe. I was knee-deep in water. I sat, or hunched, rather, bathing myself in the liquid. How on earth had I gotten here? Not with Ryan, although going under my grief had led me here. Not with Gwen, although what I felt for her — call it inspiration, call it attraction — had prodded me deeper.

I sat for a while, rocking myself in the water, letting the steam caress my face. There was nothing very beautiful about the gray walls. Even the water was dull. *Because I haven't been here in a long time.* The water, the air had grown stale. But it was the core of me. The cramped, stale core. I sighed. Around me, the rock heaved. There was nothing magical about it, but when the rock stopped shuddering, it was sort of peaceful.

As soon as I had that thought, the water surged and a wave broke over my head. I gasped, choked and kicked, trying to find the surface, clawing up for air. I wrenched myself up and out, until I was in my living room, standing by the window, panting. I ran a hand through my hair. As usual after a nightmare, waking or sleeping, I was sweaty. Drenched. That last thought had done it. There was no peace in my soul. And I wasn't eager to go back there. What was the point of sitting in the gray water alone?

There was one person I could think of who probably knew about that cracked-open place, one person who might be able to help me balance fear like a fragile water jar. It was going to take time to get up my nerve, but I needed to talk to my sister.

At seven-fifteen on Friday morning, I knocked on Gwen's door. She was up and dressed. It wouldn't be long before she was back at work. She handed me a case containing the art.

"May I come in?" I put the case on the couch and began rummaging in the kitchen. I found the eggs and bread. I'd brought orange juice. "I don't suppose you have an omelet pan?"

"It doesn't sound like something I'd know how to use. Are you planning to cook?"

"I haven't had breakfast yet."

I cracked and scrambled eggs in a saucepan, made toast, poured juice and set two plates. Her computer was on the dining table. I unplugged it. Gwen hadn't said a word but she'd made coffee and poured two mugs.

"These are good." She sampled the eggs.

"I'll make omelets next time."

"I'll be back at work next week."

"I'm glad you're feeling better." I finished eating, washed my dishes, took the art and headed out. "See you this weekend."

On Saturday, I stayed away from the office and went to the mall. On Sunday I did my housecleaning, and Sunday evening I was back at Gwen's. She let me in and I stocked her kitchen with a skillet, pepper mill, spices and assorted utensils.

She followed after me, trailing fax paper. "Andrea?"

"I'm tired of eating takeout. There's more to culinary life than stir-fry in cardboard."

"You can eat whatever you want. But you work for me, you don't live here."

"Because I work for you, I live at the office. But there's no kitchen there. From now on if we work late, I want home cooking." I pointed to the fax paper. "I don't have the right equipment at my apartment."

She inspected a pasta strainer. "I suppose you'll want to keep a toothbrush here, too?"

I didn't even blush. "Nope. I'm going to brush my teeth and say my bedtime prayers at my place."

"In other words, you're going to feed me but you don't want to fuck me." That did it. I blushed. She laughed and moved closer. "You're cute."

I put up a hand. "Don't."

She looked perplexed. "I told you I'm not contagious."

"I won't sleep with you."

She stepped back. "My mistake."

"I'm sorry if you thought I was making a pass the other night."

She gestured at the pans and spices. "Moving in, more like."

"I'm going to give you every ounce of my passion. At the office. After hours. But only in advertising."

Now her cheeks were flushed. "Well, well. Little Andy Stern has her limits."

I went home and called my mother.

She sounded relaxed. "Julia's enjoying being home," she said, as though my sister had gone on a cruise.

"Mom, can I come over?"

"Let's try a short visit next weekend. We'll see how it goes."

At my mother's house, the first thing I noticed were the pictures. Photo albums, envelopes and shoeboxes stuffed full of snapshots covered a corner desk and card table.

"Hello, Andrea." It was Saturday and Mom was dressed in a pink sweat outfit and cross-trainers.

"Hi, Mom. Are you playing tennis today?"

"No, of course not. Julia and I power-walk three miles a day."

"Wow."

"Would you like some coffee? It's decaf."

"I'd love some." She glanced at Julia and left the room. I wondered at the effort of will it took for her to leave me alone with my sister. I walked over to the card table. "Hi, sis."

"Hi, Andrea. Thanks for the letters."

"How're you doing?"

She continued to sort pictures while she talked, tossing photos into piles as though they were pieces of a jigsaw puzzle.

"The first month I was home I was doped to the gills. Don't ask me about that because I have, like, zero recall. Then Mom and I started power-walking and I cut down on my med levels. And I joined a consumer program." She said emphatically, "I feel empowered."

"I guess the exercise helps." I tried to picture myself holding weights, striding around the neighborhood. It was a short fantasy.

"Not just the workouts. The whole consumer movement. It's awesome."

"I've never heard of it."

"You used to be the smart one in the family."

"Don't be a snot. Tell me what it is before Mom gets back." I wanted to hear about her experience in her words, without Mom's editing.

"People like me are called consumers because we buy psychiatric services. We used to be called patients. I have the right to make my own treatment decisions, like what medications to take and whether or not to be hospitalized. There's a local support center."

"Are there a lot of . . . consumers?"

"Tons. It's a national movement. Mom joined a group called the Alliance. Most of them are family members, parents with schizophrenic children, people like that. They do good political stuff but they're, like, total control freaks. They can't deal with the concept that their kids can choose their own pills. Mom and I fight about it over dinner."

"This is great stuff. Can I sign up?"

She sniffed. "You're not a consumer and don't you dare join the Alliance. They think they know our rights better than we do."

"Can I make a contribution?"

"I'll give you a brochure."

Mom came into the room carrying a trivet and a coffeepot. "Andrea, the mugs are in the kitchen cabinet." As I went to get them, I heard her ask Julia, "Are you telling Andrea about your new friends?"

"Just doing a little fundraising," Julia replied. When I came back, she said, "Don't let Mom hit you up for money. You promised me, first."

"That reminds me." I retrieved a check from my hip pocket. "Car payment," I said to Julia. "I'll save my political contributions for you." I took my coffee and looked over her shoulder. "What's with the pictures?"

When I thought about my family, I plotted our lives on a timeline, subdivided by my sister's illness. There was childhood — before Julia got sick. Adolescence, my parents' divorce and the worst years of her hospitalizations came next. Then there was college for me and Julia's live-in program.

What I saw on the card table and overflowing the desk was my family the way it used to be. I was staring at my childhood, our childhood, the years that had belonged to Julia and me. A memory came back — Dad behind a camera, lining us up, making us pose. In most of the photos, though, we were natural, unposed, playing and running and swinging — Julia on a tennis court, me with a book, and the two of us together, on a picnic, in a neighbor's pool, laughing, being sisters, being children.

"Where did you get these?"

"Mom had them in a closet. They were at Grandma's when she died but no one ever put them into albums. They were all out of order." She pointed to a pile. "These are mostly you." Another pile, slightly bigger. "These are me. And these are the family vacations." As she handed me a stack of photos, her sleeve pulled and I saw the old scars on her wrist. Our eyes met. "New drugs," she whispered. "No more compulsions."

"Julia," Mom warned, "not in front of guests."

"I'm not a guest." I showed her one of the photos. "Remember me, your other kid?" She had a tight-lipped look and I could feel a fight coming on. "Do you expect Julia to wear turtlenecks all summer? Are you going to tell the neighbors that your eldest daughter joined the Peace Corps and adopted the custom of staying covered, chin to ankles?"

"Andrea, you're in my house and you will do as I say."

I put my hands on my hips. "Headline update. I'm not five anymore."

"If you're trying to tell me that you've grown up, then act like it."

"It's no wonder you're confused. You didn't spend enough time with me as a child to notice the difference in my behavior."

Mom stood up, ready to escort me out.

Julia said calmly, "Chill out, both of you. Andrea, you're my guest today. That means she's off limits to you, Mom." I almost stuck out my tongue. "Mom's afraid I'll be shunned because I was a teenage self-slasher."

There was a long silence during which Julia continued to sort pictures. Finally, Mom sat on the couch and I went back to looking at the photos.

I picked up one of the vacation shots. "I forgot about this. Remember the desert?"

"You were little."

In the photograph I was standing, sturdy and serious, next to a barrel cactus. The cactus and I were about the same height. The only vacation I'd thought about in years was the Yosemite trip, with the cliffs and waterfalls. But we'd gone to California one other time, not to the mountains but to the high desert. Looking at the pictures, I recalled wildflowers and hummingbirds. We'd hiked to an oasis, picnicked and played. At night I'd gazed into the clearest, most star-filled sky I'd ever seen, could ever remember seeing.

"I had a good time on that trip."

Julia nodded. "Me, too."

Behind me, Mom asked, "Andrea, will you stay for lunch?"

I turned, surprised to see her with her gray hair and fit figure, dressed in her sweat outfit. For a moment, I'd expected to see the woman in the photos — wavy dark hair and a dazzling smile, lean, not from working out, just from youth, wearing jeans cuffed over hiking boots.

I showed her the picture. "That's a nice shot of you. Yeah, I can stay. Do you want some help in the kitchen?"

"That's all right. Julia, why don't you show Andrea your room."

Mom's new house had two bedrooms, an office and an outdoor patio. I disagreed with Dad's assumption that it was like the home I'd grown up in. It was smaller, for starters, and less pretentious. The dining-room table, for example, was ash, lightly stained to bring out the wood's blond color. It seated six, a far cry from the drop-leaf monstrosity I'd hidden under as a child.

The walls in Julia's room were hung with the prints I'd sent.

"I guess you have enough pictures."

"I like them." She picked up a remote and activated an expensive sound system, then flopped onto the bed. "I'm worried about Mom."

I joined her on the bed. "She exudes success."

"Except for work, she doesn't go out. I mean, not at all. She comes straight home like I'm a pet that needs to be let out. And she calls at lunch. She calls all the time."

"Is she worried that you're home alone?"

"I get home about twenty minutes before she does. When I'm not in day-treatment, I'm at the consumer center. And I see my shrink, Dr. Meadows, every week. Mom has all the phone numbers. It drives me crazy." She rolled on her back. "She thinks if she's a good parent, I'll get better. I won't. Not her way."

I scooted up and lay down. "Are you sure it was a good idea to come home?"

"She has to get a life," Julia said. "I'm not gonna live with her forever."

"Are you going to get your own place?"

"Someday."

"Live with me." There it was again, that strange

request. Some part of me couldn't believe that ten years had passed. I still thought of us as thirteen and sixteen. I was making plans for us to grow up and room together. "I work late and I won't call at lunch. You can have your privacy."

"Do you mean it?"

"About working late? Yeah. I'm never home."

She punched my arm. "We'd fight."

"So what? We were practically separated at birth —"

"Adolescence."

"I could stand to have a fight about who cleans the bathroom."

"We spent our entire childhood fighting."

I thought about that. "Did we hate each other?"

"No, but we didn't learn to love each other, either. We had shitty role modeling." She folded her arms. "Mom treats me like I'm still sixteen. I know the side effects and toxic levels of my drugs better than the doctors." She turned her head to look at me. "I'm twenty-six and I've never had a job."

"Mom thinks you need stability."

"She's afraid I'll do another attempt. She acts like I'm a hand grenade. When she calls, she says, 'How is everything?' What she really wants to know is, 'Is your pin still in?' Like it'll drop out and I'll explode."

Julia had a butterfly poster taped to the ceiling. The names of each species underlined the pictures.

"Do you think you will, ever?"

"Say it like *Jeopardy*."

"What?"

"The TV show. Ask it like that."

"I don't watch that show." She closed her eyes, ignoring me. I said, "Um, death by your own hand?"

Her eyes flew open. "What is suicide!"

"So, are you going to or what?"

She leaned over and whispered, "You're wired, right? Mom sent you in here with a tape recorder, didn't she?" She grabbed me around the ribs and started to tickle.

I howled. "Stop. Stop it. Oh, God, okay. I'm sorry. Julia, I'm sorry!"

She released me. "Wimp."

"Am not."

"Are too." She eyed me. "Would you really let me live with you?"

"Sure. As long as Mom pays your share of the rent."

I propped myself on an elbow. Julia was wearing baggy jeans and a loose, high-collared, long-sleeved shirt that covered the scars on her wrists and neck. Her hair was clean, cut to the shoulders. It was straighter than mine, like Mom's. I had our father's curls. Her face was half in shadow, half in sun. I thought her beautiful.

She asked, "How come it took you so long to come home?"

"Mom told me to stay away."

"And you let her? Dummy. How much did you get out of her?"

"You know about Dad?"

"He sneaks around the consumer center like some kind of vitamin guru. He thinks he's so cool. You want to know something weird? He joined the parents' group first."

"Dad's in a support group?"

"That's how Mom found out about it. They go to separate meetings, though."

"He should pay his share."

"She makes more money."

I said, "She helped me buy a car. But the real reason I wasn't around is because I had some personal stuff to deal with."

"You mean coming out?"

"You know I'm gay?"

"It was obvious when you were six. You were such a tomboy."

"I was a bookworm. You were into sports."

"I played tennis. I wore dresses."

"Tennis, right. No lesbians in that sport."

"You spent your entire childhood in brown corduroy pants. If that's not queer, what is?"

"You should've enlightened me. I never even kissed a girl until college. I knew earlier," I admitted. "I wrote a paper."

"Skip the paper. Tell me about your girlfriends."

"In high school, I saw two girls together in the locker room. I hated gym, so I always waited for the tardy bell. They were necking."

"Did they see you?"

"Hard not to. I crashed into a locker and practically knocked myself out."

"Klutz."

"One of them yelled, 'Get her!' The other one said, 'Forget it. She's one too and doesn't know it yet.' They went back to kissing and I kept staring. Then the first one said, 'Get your own,' and they laughed and I ran off."

"That's your coming-out story? How pathetic. Know what I would have done? I would've grabbed the first one and said, 'Shove over.' "

"You've had more assertiveness training."

"That's for sure."

"Have you ever — ?"

"Kissed a girl? Nope. I like guys." She looked suddenly fearful. "Don't tell Mom. There's a guy from the live-in program. We started dating after I left."

"How come you don't want Mom to know?"

"He's a counselor."

"That's unethical, right?"

"I told you, we waited until I moved out."

I thought back to my Women's Studies class. "Aren't you afraid of, you know, power dynamics?"

"Matt's okay."

"Well, don't let him take advantage. And don't have unprotected sex."

"We're not doing that yet."

"Do you want to borrow my copy of *Our Bodies, Ourselves*?"

Julia said to the ceiling, "What did I do to deserve such a square sister?" She smiled sweetly. "If he tries anything, I'll get a razor and slice his nuts." I roared. She cranked the volume on the CD player. "Shh. I don't want Mom to hear."

When I stopped laughing, I said, "I had a girlfriend in college. It was pretty serious."

"Did you break up?"

"She died."

Julia touched my arm. "I'm sorry. What happened?"

"She was an incredible athlete. I mean, she was probably going to the Olympics for track and field. That's how good she was. And she would have gone to graduate school, seminary, because she wanted to be a priest. But her heart stopped."

"What was her name?"

"Ryan."

"You loved her, huh?"

"Yeah." I blinked a few times to clear my eyes. "I was mad at myself for not seeing that something was wrong. Her doctor didn't know, either. But I should have."

Julia said, "I used to really hate Mom and Dad for making me schizo."

"Get over it. Ryan had a bad heart. Her parents didn't intentionally screw wrong to give her bad genes. It's not like Mom and Dad went to bed and said, 'Let's fuck, and fuck up our children while we're at it.'"

"Easy for you to say. You're not crazy."

"Right. I'm queer."

"You're jealous."

"What?"

"Admit it. If it weren't for me being psycho, you'd get more attention for being gay. Mom and Dad are like, 'Well, your head still works, so don't bother us about the other stuff.' You're on your own for sexual orientation."

I sighed. "It kind of sucks."

"I'm really sorry about your girlfriend."

We'd rolled toward each other. "Julia? I love you."

"I love you, too."

After a while, I said, "What do you think Mom is doing? She was going to make lunch and that was almost an hour ago."

"She's giving us space. Before you got here, I told her I needed private time with my sister."

I said admiringly, "You're good. You know what? I always thought she blamed me because you were sick.

If she could have picked, she would have had me be crazy."

"That's just transference. She's pissed at Dad, so she takes it out on you. He was a bad husband and you got voted in as the bad daughter. I was supposed to be the perfect daughter. She's trying, though. She's in therapy."

I pictured Mom in her sweat outfit and cross-trainers, using a tennis racquet to beat up a therapist's couch while screaming, "I hate my family!"

"She doesn't know how scared I am," Julia said softly. "You can't imagine how awful it is. People tiptoeing around, expecting me to fall apart, trying not to look and dying to know if there's a new scar. They always ask, 'Are you okay?' I want to say, 'No. I'm not.' Without the drugs, I'd probably hurt myself. What nobody understands is, for me, that's normal. I'm so close to the place where reality gets thin." She nudged me. "Do you remember when we were kids and we had summer art classes?"

"You did art, I took science." I stared at the poster on the ceiling. "I was supposed to make a butterfly collection and Mom caught them all for me. It was fun, though, doing it with her."

"They had this stuff, rice paper, I think, and we painted it to look like lanterns. That's what reality feels like to me — thin and crinkly. Sometimes I get this feeling like it's going to tear." She put her hands over her face. When she took them away, I studied her skin. She had the barest hint of wrinkles around her eyes. The creases beside her mouth were more pronounced than mine. She whispered, "I'm so afraid I'm gonna lose it again."

I said, "I'm not worried about something

happening to me. Just everyone else. I used to have this nightmare that Dad fell off a cliff."

"Creepy."

"I get scared that stuff is going to happen. War. Famine. Heart attacks." I asked the question that I'd come to ask. "How do you deal with it?"

"Drugs."

"Julia —"

"What's the matter with you? Do you have a phobia of natural disasters?"

"Not the disaster and destruction part. Just death."

"Well, if it happens all of a sudden, you're lucky. It's the slow part that's hard. Fighting the urges. Knowing it's wrong, and then not knowing. Getting suckered by the insanity. Being afraid to die isn't a problem. Wanting it is."

I was listening closely. I asked hopefully, "So you're saying my fear is normal?"

"You're totally neurotic, but it runs in the family."

"I already know that. Mom and Dad are terrified of losing you."

"It's time to cope. I need to get on with my life. I want my own apartment."

"Me, too."

"I thought you had your own place."

"That doesn't mean I have a life." After a while, I asked, "Are you ready for lunch?"

"Not yet."

We lay on our backs, staring at the ceiling butterflies.

Chapter 14

It was Saturday night and I couldn't settle down. After lunch, as I was leaving, Julia had pushed an envelope into my hands. "This is your batch."

I turned on a lamp and sorted through the snapshots. My sister, the historian, had made me a gift of family photos, and with them came a sense of perspective. Time had opened, expanded. Before today, the bulk of my life had been about Ryan. Now that joy-filled, pain-racked year was sandwiched firmly between a past that included my parents, a future that included Julia. All of a sudden, people were sprouting up around me like stalks of corn.

I'd given up a Saturday at the office to see Julia, and I found myself thinking about Gwen. I put the pictures away and picked up the phone. A woman's voice, not Gwen's, answered.

"Is Gwen there?"

"Hang on." I heard music. "Hey, babe. Get the phone."

I hung up. I didn't even have the energy to swear. I was drained — from the day's drive, the family visit, the tension that lingered between Mom and me, and from the effort to get to know Julia again. And all the memories — so many photos' worth. It was too much. I showered and got ready for bed. I felt gypped, cheated, hoaxed. Just when time had started to move again for me, Gwen had moved on. Fleetingly, I wondered where she'd found her. At a party? In a bar?

"Slut." I spat the word, angry at being alone, angry at Gwen because she wasn't. "You still love Ryan," I whispered.

Ryan's not here right now, is she?

At dawn, I got up and made coffee. I had one advantage over anyone else who was seeing Gwen. I wrote for her. I dug around for some notebook paper, remembering a literature course I'd taken that had been taught by a tough, elderly professor.

"There is writing and there is literature." She had faced the class. "Who can tell the difference?"

"Literature uses symbolism," someone ventured.

"As do Superman comics," she tossed back, to loud cheers.

"Different levels of meaning," another student guessed.

"You mean literature is a lamp with a three-way switch?"

"It uses simile and metaphor," came an astute observation.

"So do clever advertisements," she admonished. "Is this all we know?" She singled me out. "The quiet one. Would you care to guess?"

It was early in spring semester. When Ryan and I weren't studying or arguing, we were making love. I thought about our endless conversations, her faith and my skepticism.

I said, "I think literature is like religion. It touches people in different ways."

"Go on. You and I read the same novel or listen to the same sermon and each of us is stimulated to different thought. Is the message profound, or merely unfocused?" The class laughed and she clapped. "Let the acolyte answer."

I should have been rapt but part of my mind refused to stay in the classroom. Diverted, my attention wandered to Ryan, our arms and legs entwined, mouths open, her tongue subduing mine. I wriggled, pinned by the professor's finger. "Um, the story feels different because each reader has different emotions."

Her hands dropped and her gaze caught each student in turn. "Do you understand? The story makes us feel, not just the fiction but our selves. We enter into it and it changes us, no two in a similar way. One story, infinite variations of emotional response." She waved us out of the classroom. "Read for it. Get involved with the literature."

Someone grumbled, "Is that homework?"

She had overheard and snapped, "It's the assignment for the rest of your lives."

I made more coffee and began to scribble. I started to write about Ryan but halfway through it changed and I was writing about Gwen. One story. Infinite emotional response. I closed the notebook.

On Monday, I was late for work. I sat at my desk and stared blearily at my copy. Nothing made sense. Worse, when it did become clear, I thought it was terrible.

Gwen walked up while I was highlighting blocks of text. "Where's Rest-Fit?"

"Right here." She wanted the mattress ad. I hit the delete key.

She blinked. "Did you just delete the copy that's due this morning?"

"Yeah."

"Get it back."

"Can't."

"Move over." She clicked on the restore sequence and retrieved the back-up file.

I said, "It stinks."

"What happened to you this weekend?"

"Nothing. Why?"

"You look like you have a hangover." She printed a hard copy and scanned it. "This is fine."

"It sucks."

"Are you sick?"

"Yeah. Sick and tired of writing this crap."

She stared hard at me. "Go home."

"Huh?"

"You heard me. Get out of here."

At home I went back to my notebook, writing in

fits and starts, grinding my way through one horrible paragraph after another. The words were full of static, sticking to one another, jamming together, balling up and refusing to flow. After a while it was just too painful. I stopped writing and opened a beer. I had the desire to express myself through words but seemingly not the ability. And my job — God, what was the point in that? I contemplated my beer. I'd stocked Gwen's kitchen and promised to cook. But if I couldn't write for her, I had no excuse to feed her. I didn't even have that.

At seven o'clock, I opened my door to her knock. Her leather jacket was slung over one arm, a pizza box balanced on the other.

She stepped inside and looked around. "I got your address from personnel. I hope you don't mind." She tossed her bangs back. "Are you hungry?"

I tried to remember lunch. Beer and crackers. "Maybe." She was still in her work clothes — a skirt and short-sleeved sweater. Her skimpy outfits never made her look gangly, just gorgeous. She kicked her shoes off and deposited the pizza on my kitchen counter. I didn't mind that she was making herself comfortable. "Do you want a beer?"

"No, thanks." She opened my refrigerator and helped herself to orange juice.

I poured juice for myself and followed her back to the living room. She zeroed in on the folder of looseleaf pages, drawn to my writing like metal shavings to a magnet. I kept quiet. If she could read my handwriting, which I doubted, then she'd see me for what I was — an amateur without the guts to convey real emotion. I was a miserable writer and when she saw it, she'd fire me and go away. Maybe she'd leave the pizza as severance pay. I sipped my juice.

Finally, she said, "I thought so." She was reading the part where I'd been writing about Ryan. I'd tried to describe the lake, the water's silver sheen and the powder-blue sky. I'd failed by a mile to capture a hint of its beauty. She asked, "Is this about your lover, the one who died?"

I nodded and reached for the folder before she got to the pages where I'd tried to describe her. Enough was enough. "It's pretty awful. I guess I'll keep my day job." I remembered that she'd sent me home. "Do I still have a job?"

"Do you mind if we eat? I'm starving." I fetched plates and the pizza and Gwen tucked her feet up on my secondhand sofa. She said, "Let me guess. Yesterday you decided to write a novel."

"I was just trying to describe some feelings." That I'd even attempted it embarrassed me beyond measure.

"And today you concluded that everything you've ever written is for shit."

"Well, yeah." The pizza was olive and tomato. Very garlicky. I licked my fingers.

"Do you think you're the first person in advertising to dabble in fine arts? Everyone's got a notebook or a sketchpad in their desk, a canvas in the spare bedroom."

"What about you?"

"Not so much since I got into management. That's why it's fun to draw for you." She smiled and her eyes looked soft. "If you want to write stories, go ahead. If you want to quit your job, I won't stop you. Just don't confuse the two." The softness disappeared. "And if you ever delete copy on deadline again, I'll dismember you." She finished eating, set her plate aside and stretched. "Did you think all those ads you've been doing were lost on me? Even Casper noticed."

I swallowed with difficulty. The good news was I still had a job. But I was dismally transparent. "What did Casper say?"

"Something about not being able to dredge it out of you." She grinned. "I'm the one who got it."

When she bent close, I flinched. I got up and cleared our plates. Gwen stayed seated, legs crossed, hands in her lap.

When I came out of the kitchen, I kept my distance. "I didn't think I was your type."

"To be honest, you're not." She made a show of inspecting me, her gaze raking up and down my body. But she had that soft look again. Usually her features were sharp, but tonight the edges seemed blurred, as though an artist had drawn her portrait and smudged the lines. "Andrea, you've been flirting with me. I love it that you're a soft sell, but we can't go on like this." When I didn't move, she got up and scooped up the leftover pizza. "You should wrap this." She carried the box into the kitchen.

I moved to the window, waiting for her to finish and leave, waiting for my monster to come writhing through the walls. I heard cupboards opening and something shattered.

Gwen said, "Damn." I hurried to the kitchen. "I can't find tinfoil, and I need a broom."

"Careful. Come over here." I held out a hand, helped her step across the broken glass. She was still in stocking feet.

"Sorry about that. I'll get you a new set."

"It was a jelly jar. Easy to replace."

I fetched the broom and dustpan. I had my boots on and swept up the debris. Gwen watched while I stowed the leftovers in the fridge. The pizza box went into the trash and I tied the bag, washed my hands.

Gwen turned away and picked up her jacket. "You're a good writer, Andrea. Come back to work tomorrow."

She'd done what she could. Fed me, complimented me. It was like singing praises from the rooftop.

She's in it for the ads, I reminded myself. But she'd called my bluff. "Why don't you stay," I heard myself say.

She dropped her jacket.

This time when she bent to me, I didn't pull away. Her lips were soft, like her eyes. I reached up, to touch her chest. Suddenly I realized what I was doing. This was Gwen. My boss. Gwen the bitch. What made me think I could get inside her? What made me want to?

I drew back. "I'm not very good at sharing." My jaw ached. "You're already seeing someone."

She caught my arm. "It was you on Saturday. You called and hung up."

"You had company."

"You little jerk." Her eyes were obsidian.

"Tell me I'm wrong." I didn't care about Gwen's dating ethics but in my confusion I was picking a fight.

"Not that I owe you an explanation, but the woman who answered my phone is my personal

196

trainer. When you called, I was in the middle of abdominal crunches."

"She called you 'babe.' "

"You should hear what she calls me when I can't finish a set. Do you think I want to spend my Saturday nights doing sit-ups? I had a heart attack. I gave up alcohol and cigarettes, for Christ's sake." Her eyes were glinting, but not from anger. Her tears caught my attention. She said, "Some survivors are grateful, as though life is new and precious. I hate it that I lost my life, and I still don't feel like I've got all of it back. Something important got sucked away when they drained the fluid out of my heart. It's unbearable. You can't imagine."

I could imagine all too well what it felt like to lose something precious and irreplaceable. I said, "The one and only lover I've ever had died of a heart attack. Given your situation, you should probably avoid me like tobacco."

She touched my temple, sweeping back a lock of hair. "Take your clothes off." She kissed me.

With effort, I separated my lips from hers. "Don't you want to go into the bedroom?"

"I'm afraid you'll change what passes for your mind. Get naked."

I stripped. Spring was still cold and my apartment was chilly. Gwen located the thermostat and turned up the heat. Then she removed her clothes. Her stomach was flat, probably from all the crunches. In spite of her workouts, she was smooth, not muscular. Undressed, her curves showed — swelling hips, her full breasts a fraction uneven. She shivered when I touched her.

I said, "Let's get in bed."

"I want to do it here, right now."

"The couch at least." I led her and we sank down.

Her hands were on my back. She cupped my ass, then slid a hand between my legs. I tensed.

She groaned. "Don't you dare stop this."

Memory is never accurate. Had I seen Ryan after those long years, I might have been surprised to find that her hair was lighter than I remembered, or darker, her eyes a different shade of blue. With Gwen beneath me, I couldn't see Ryan at all. For the first time since her death, I was glad.

I lay on Gwen, getting lost in her kisses. I found her breasts and fondled them, then suckled. She was touching me, too, but her legs opened first. I clasped her hips and hesitated.

"Andrea." Her voice was hoarse. "Do it." I went all the way down. When she was finished she pulled me up, gripped my thigh between hers. She murmured, "You're good."

When her shudders had quieted, I went to the bedroom and bundled up my comforter. I shut the lights and covered us. She moved languidly, nipping my breasts and fingering my mound. Gently, she stroked me open.

When my hips began to move, she whispered, "Do you want me inside?"

My breath caught. "Yeah."

She went up in me. It was dark but I knew she was watching, paying attention to the way I angled, letting me rub and move on her, all the while stroking me inside. I came faster than I expected, more wetly than I remembered.

She laughed softly, eased out and palmed my back. I was shaking. She asked, "You okay?"

I shifted, lay beside her. "Thanks." It sounded so inadequate. "You're beautiful."

She wrapped her arms loosely around my shoulders. "We're not done."

Only when she had a kink in her neck and I'd fallen off the couch did she let me coax her into the bedroom.

"Are you afraid if we get comfortable we'll have to stop?"

"I can't remember what I'm afraid of," she said.

I stopped holding back. During the night, I stopped caring if she knew how desperate I was to touch and be touched. I stopped worrying that it showed. I was afraid that in the morning she'd change her mind, decide she'd had her fill and could do without sex. Maybe I'd whet her appetite and then fail to satisfy it. What if, for all our lovemaking, she wanted someone else? I put my lips on her, felt hers on me, and concentrated on making her come.

It was still dark when she dressed and left. I set my alarm and slept for an hour, then showered, dressed and went to work. She came in before anyone else, so I brought her a mug of coffee.

"Thanks." She handed me a file. "I need this tonight. Can you work late?"

"Sure. Are you hungry? I'll go to the bakery."

"No, thanks." I turned to go. "Andrea? Lunch at my place?"

"I'll meet you there."

We made love on top of her bed without getting under the covers. I glanced longingly at her kitchen and bought takeout burritos on the way back to work.

That night she slept over. In the morning, we showered together. I watched her while she shampooed her hair.

She opened her eyes and caught me staring. "What is it?"

"No scars?"

"They used a needle to drain the fluid caused by the infection. They didn't have to cut me open."

"Oh." I kept staring.

"Anything else?"

I shook my head.

She stepped out of the shower and grabbed a towel. By the time I dried myself and came into the bedroom, she had her skirt and bra on and was buttoning her blouse. I sat on the bed and watched.

She searched through my dresser, found a rugby shirt and threw it at me.

"Top drawer. Undershirt." I snagged it as it sailed past. Half-dressed, I said, "My scars don't show either."

She stepped into her shoes and touched my cheek. "They're bigger than you are."

I padded after her to the door. "I'm sorry I was staring. I was wondering what you look like . . . on the inside."

She bent to kiss me. "You are so weird. See you at work."

I rushed to finish dressing.

Chapter 15

During the next couple of months, I continued to write all of my copy specifically for Gwen. She'd reached a compromise with the rest of the staff — quality work without ungodly hours. Casper was still upstairs. As far as I knew, her plans to replace him were proceeding but she kept silent on that score. We often worked late but went home for dinner, either to her place or mine. We slept together, showered together and drove to work separately.

On Saturdays our routine was much the same, except we went to work a little later and didn't stay as long. On Saturday night I cooked more elaborately. We stayed in by choice. For me it was a natural inclination. Gwen wanted to keep our relationship quiet.

"Don't you think people will notice?" I asked.

"I don't care if they see us working. I don't want to advertise our personal relationship."

"They're bound to gossip."

"The consensus is that I'm inhuman and you're trying to score merit points."

"That reminds me. About my raise —"

She swatted my bottom.

The only night we didn't spend together was Sunday. On Sunday morning we slept late, ate brunch and read the newspaper in bed. Then, by unspoken agreement, the one visiting returned home. On those sleepy mornings we made love slowly, as though to ward off the upcoming solitary night.

In the afternoon I did laundry, bought groceries, paid bills and puttered around. It was a time reserved for family and I spent it alone. I'd never been with Ryan on Sunday, either. She'd been with her family, at church.

"Are you glad for me?" I whispered. "Or do you hate me for betraying you?" I knew Ryan would never hate me. The June weather was warm and I had my window propped open. The curtains stirred. I put my head against the sill and yelled, "Talk to me!" My outburst startled a passerby. The phone rang. Breathless, I picked it up. "Hello?"

"Hi. It's Julia."

"Oh. Hi."

"You sound disappointed. Who were you expecting?"

"No one. How's it going?"

"Like crap. Mom won't even talk about letting me get my own place. She's totally flipped out. I need your help."

"She won't listen to me."

"I'm going to look for an apartment. Matt wants to come but he'll say yes to anything."

"Matt?"

"You know, the guy from the live-in program."

"Oh, you mean the counselor you're dating. No, don't go with him. I'll take you." I was flattered that she'd asked. "Have you worked out the finances?"

"Don't depress me."

"Does Mom know about Matt?"

"She thinks he's from the support center."

"Um, that makes him a social worker masquerading as a patient, I mean consumer."

"These are my politics, not yours."

"Is he good enough for you?"

"He's got, like, no boundaries, and I'm schizophrenic. I'd say we both have self-esteem issues. I need you to stay focused on apartments. Let's go next weekend."

I thought about my schedule. "I usually work on Saturdays."

After a silence, she said, "Dad worked every Saturday. Remember?"

I remembered Julia and Mom at tennis tournaments, Dad at the office, me at Grandma's. I thought about Gwen. "I'll come Sunday afternoon."

"I'll call you back."

She called midweek. I was in the kitchen waiting for a pot of rice to finish cooking. Gwen was on the couch, dozing under the newspaper. It was eight o'clock and I was thinking seriously about ditching dinner and dragging her to bed.

"Hi, Andrea. I have three places lined up for Saturday."

"I thought we agreed on Sunday."

Gwen surfaced from the newspaper and peered blearily at the phone.

Julia said, "Matt has Sunday off. We're going to a matinee."

Gwen closed her eyes. She looked sexy and tired. We were both working too hard. Worse, we were reluctant to simply sleep together, as though our physical relationship were the only reason to spend the night. I was beginning to crave a different kind of intimacy, a way of being together that had nothing to do with sex.

I said, "Saturday's fine. I'll pick you up."

"Mom says you're invited for lunch." She lowered her voice. "She thinks we're going to the mall."

Gwen was watching me again, looking more alert.

"I have to go to the office first." The drive to Worcester took an hour. "I'll try to get there by one."

When I hung up, Gwen asked, "Are you keeping a girlfriend on the side? Where do you find the energy?"

"My sister wants to go apartment-hunting." I went back to my cooking. The rice was done and I began heating oil for a stir-fry. Gwen came into the kitchen. "Let's take Saturday off," I suggested. "We can sleep late, go out to breakfast."

"No. I mean, sure. You deserve a break. I have to work."

I wasn't paying attention and dumped wet vegetables into the over-heated wok. Hot oil splattered. "Shit." I grabbed the pan off the heat and sucked on a burn.

"Let me see." She reached for my hand.

"Don't." I jerked away.

She poked a spoon into the oil-soaked vegetables. "Let's go to bed."

"You go. I'll clean up." I turned on the tap, letting the cold water soothe my fingers.

Gwen snapped, "What's the matter with you? I'm not forcing you to work on Saturday." I shut off the water, no longer caring if she saw that I was about to cry. She looked concerned. "Does it hurt that much?"

It took me a minute to realize she meant my hand. "It hurts," I yelled, "but not because I burned myself."

She stalked out of the kitchen. "I don't need this."

I ran after her. "You don't need anything but work on deadline and a good fuck every night." I wasn't going to let her go without a fight.

She bit down on her temper. "I'm too tired for tantrums."

My stomach hurt from trying to hold the tears in. I made it to the couch. She paced to the door, clearly battling the urge to flee, then took up a stance in front of me, her arms crossed. It made me think of all the time she spent upstairs at the office, hashing deals with the partners.

She watched me cry, then sat beside me. "What's this about?"

"I want us to do something besides work and have sex." She stroked the tears from my face. I said, "This isn't going to work for us, is it?"

"It's not about sex, Andrea. Do you really think I'm using you that badly? For work and a good time?" It was hard for me to meet her eyes. "Do you?"

"No," I mumbled. "I don't know why you hang out with me."

"Well, you're cute."

"Don't tease."

"You're a good cook."

"Cut it out." But she'd made me smile. I grumbled, "I screwed up the stir-fry."

"I'm sorry if I made you feel like I was coming around to be catered to. The truth is, I was interested in you from the moment I saw you crying in that awful bar. You're so close to your pain." She sighed. "I haven't been involved with anyone in a long time. I was never very good at it."

Grudgingly, I said, "You're pretty good."

"I've never been close to anyone the way you have." She held my face, compelled me to look at her. "Something happened to you when she died. What was it?"

Slowly, I described my vision, the utterly real yet transparent manifestation I'd seen in the moments before Ryan's death. "I was in the library. It got really cold and I saw her standing in front of me. I thought she'd gotten out of practice early but then I could see that something was wrong." My next words came out flat, hollow-sounding. "She didn't have a heart. I could see into her chest and her heart was gone." Beside me, Gwen stirred. She was crying. "What did you see," I whispered, "when it happened to you?"

She wiped her tears. "The usual. White lights. It was like watching myself from far away, like looking through the wrong end of a telescope. Everything was small, distant. I didn't know I was in trouble until I looked down. I had this awful sensation that I couldn't get back." She stopped talking.

I said, "I thought near-death experiences were supposed to be pleasant."

"It was like a camera shutter closing — everything got dark. I saw a light, like everyone says, and then a hand came out and I felt myself moving. I woke up on the table. I've never been religious but I started praying, pleading to stay put. The light got closer and it felt like there was a hand on my chest, holding me down."

"Through the veil. That's how Ryan described it. She believed you could go from the physical to the spiritual."

Gwen said, "I feel like part of me is still outside, hovering. I'm afraid I'll wake up one day on the ceiling — out there again, apart from my life."

Something was happening in the pit of my stomach. There was a flow starting, like a stream building, swelling within its banks. And my chest cavity was filling — not with fluid, not from pneumonia, but with buoyant light. I reached for Gwen. She was close, so close to my touch.

She whispered, "I can't compete with wings and halos."

"I know she's gone."

"Do you?" She ran a hand through her hair. "I need a shower." She got up and headed for the bathroom.

I cleaned up the dinner mess, went into the bathroom and got undressed. Gwen was still in the shower so I stuck my head around the curtain. "May I join you?"

She drew me in.

When we got into bed, I held her and wondered if I'd ever be able to feel and see another person the way I'd had Ryan. I tried to remember what she'd taught me about faith, but I had no dreams that night, no inspiration.

On Saturday, I picked up Julia in Worcester and drove to the first apartment. It was one room in an old house, not a full kitchen, just a hot plate. The windows were painted shut. I'd brought my flashlight and yanked open a closet.

"Come on. What's next on the list?"

"What's wrong? What's in there?"

"Cockroaches." I glared at the landlady and put a protective arm around Julia.

The next two places were variations on a theme — single rooms, bathroom down the hall, chipped paint under layers of grime, and various fire hazards.

Julia was close to tears. "Everything is so gross." She tossed the classifieds at me. "You find one."

I scanned the ads. "For my apartment, I pay more than twice what these cost. That's not including first and last month and a deposit."

Julia pulled a notebook and pen from her shoulder bag and went over a list of scrawled phone numbers and dollar amounts. "I can get assistance for my medication and subsidized housing. The waiting list for a single person, no children, is two years. Or I can go off my meds and live with roaches."

"Don't stop taking the medicine."

"Either way, I still need Mom's money."

"Live with me." I didn't know why the idea had so much appeal. I'd never lived in a dorm and I was having some kind of pajama-party fantasy. Having a roommate would probably cramp my love life. On the other hand, once Julia stopped worrying about keeping her scars covered, it was easy to imagine her and Gwen sharing clothes.

"Are you inviting me with or without Mom?"

"She's not disinheriting you. She'll help you pay for a decent place."

"She wants me to stay with her forever." Panic was close to the surface. "Let's go back and look at the first one."

"It was full of roaches."

"Just drive, okay?"

"And take you where? To live in a firetrap? I thought you weren't self-destructive anymore." I clamped my lips. "Shit. What a stupid thing to say."

Julia pounded the back of her head against the headrest. "They totally don't prepare you for this. The supervised program wasn't anything like the real world." Tears gathered on her lashes. "I can't support myself."

"Can't you get training or something?"

"I can go for my high school equivalency." She

turned her head to look at me. "What if I can't do it, Andrea? I was in high school when I lost it. What if I can't handle it?"

"Do what you know and fake the rest. That's what everyone does."

"Do you fake it?"

I thought about my incomplete college career, the ads I wrote for Gwen. "I used to. Not so much anymore."

"I have to pretend to be cool around Mom. If she knew what a basket case I am, she'd never let me out of the house. She wants me to work for her as a part-time file clerk." She held up a hand. "Before you ask, the answer is no. I did enough psychodrama when I was in the hospital." She crossed her arms. "My life is useless. I never even got my driver's license."

"You're not useless," I said vehemently. "I'll teach you to drive. All we need is an empty parking lot." We found our way to the city Y as the lot was emptying for the supper hour.

Julia asked, "Is this legal? Don't I need a learner's permit?"

"Um, not for your first lesson."

"That's what I like about you. You make things up."

It was a silly, wonderful thing for her to say. We smiled at each other over the top of the car, then walked around and switched seats.

"This is a little complicated because I have standard transmission. What's Mom driving these days?"

"Something expensive. A Lexus, I think."

"We'll start with this." She popped the clutch until we were rattled. I said, "Slow. Let it out slow."

"I think I've got it."

"Okay, give it some gas."

She stomped the accelerator and the car surged and bucked.

"I'm getting the hang of it. Can I take it around the block?"

"Next lesson." After a few turns around the parking lot, I drove us to Mom's. The Lexus was in the driveway and I peered through the window.

"What are you so happy about?"

I was grinning. "Automatic transmission. Let's get some practice asking for the car keys."

We raced each other inside. Mom invited me to stay for dinner. I declined.

Julia asked, "Why not?"

"I'm getting together with someone."

"You have a new girlfriend, don't you?"

Mom was holding a salad spinner. "Oh? What's her name?"

"Gwen."

"Would you like to bring her for dinner some night? Julia can invite one of her friends."

"I'll ask her."

"Come early," Julia said. "I want another driving lesson."

Mom started up the salad spinner. The lettuce was going to be very dry.

When I got home, I called Gwen. "Did you have dinner yet?"

"I was just looking in the freezer."

"No. Not the freezer. I'll be right over."

She watched me pour beaten eggs into a skillet. When the edges were done and the middle was bubbling, I added cheese and ground pepper. I began slicing tomatoes.

"Is your mother a good cook?"

"She's a gourmet. I cook like a peasant."

"You underestimate yourself. How'd it go today?"

"No apartments. I gave her a driving lesson."

"Beyond the call of sisterly duty."

"We're invited to dinner sometime." I turned the eggs out of the pan and tried to sound casual. "Want to go?"

She moved into the dining room, set the table and lit a pair of candles. Instantly, the room looked elegant. It had been a long time since I'd dined by candlelight. When I left New Hampshire, I'd packed my grandmother's candlesticks and they'd been in the back of a kitchen drawer ever since. Standing in the light, Gwen looked radiant. "It was sweet of you to come over and cook. You've had a long day."

"I wanted to see you."

When we were seated, she asked, "Who's going to be at this get-together?"

"My mother, sister and my sister's boyfriend. Julia's schizophrenic," I said neutrally. "She was in a halfway program and now she's living with Mom." I concentrated on my dinner. "I've never brought a girlfriend home before. Maybe we should skip it."

Under the table, Gwen's shoeless foot caressed my shin. "Don't you want me to meet your family?"

"Promise you won't break up with me when you see how nuts they are."

"Cross my heart."

"Don't say that. Don't you know the rest of the rhyme?"

"Cross my heart, hope to die, stick a needle in my eye."

I was aghast. "You can't say that."

"Andrea? What's wrong?"

I was no longer staring at Gwen, but at the liquid shadow that had appeared at her shoulder. It was as though her shadow, cast by the candlelight, had been swept off the floor, the way wind in the desert blows sand into a whirling funnel, a dust-devil. The shadow-devil stood behind her, cloaked and menacing. It wasn't hard to imagine crossed arms, heavy shoulders, a brooding brow. It lacked the cuddly familiarity of my fear-monster. This was no leftover childhood nightmare but a hulking, adult terror. When Gwen stood up, the shadow separated from her. She led me to the sofa and tried to soothe me, smoothing my goosepimpled skin. The devil took up a station in the corner.

At that moment, I lost all hope of love.

After Ryan died, I thought I'd never be tempted. With Gwen, I'd come close. But I couldn't get away from the terror, the foul entity that preyed on me. Here it was in Gwen's living room, picking razorblade teeth. I'd never be able to love someone without the monstrous fear of losing them always lurking.

"Gwen?" I kept my voice low so the shadow wouldn't hear.

"Mmm?" She had her arms around me.

"I'm afraid." In my head, a noise like a chainsaw

started up. It was the shadow-devil laughing. I spoke through the racket. "I don't want anything bad to happen to you."

She said, "If I could sink a grappling hook into my ribs and tie it to something — my desk, my car, you — I'd do it. But I think you'd get tired of dragging me around."

"I'll hold you."

"You can't hold onto me any more than you could hang onto your ex. Andrea, you have to stop trying. Let go."

Let go of what? I wanted to scream. The one love that was supposed to last forever? Or the exasperated woman sitting next to me? The fear of losing Gwen — not to death but to my own inadequacy — drenched me.

"What do I have to do?" I whispered.

"Stop acting like I'm going to get hit by a bus. It's getting on my nerves."

Behind the shadow, a golden form appeared. In Gwen's living room, the two sides squared off — Ryan, strong and brave, and the devilish fear.

It's a stand-off, I thought.

Gwen pulled me to my feet and led me to the bathroom. We washed and got ready for bed. As she settled in beside me, I had a sense that the balance had tipped. In my mind, a glowing hand had a stranglehold on the shadow.

Chapter 16

Several weeks later, I took Gwen to meet my family. A young man wearing a black polo shirt and red suspenders opened Mom's door. Matt, I presumed. He was growing a goatee, which he looked about thirty years too young for. Summer was progressing and I'd switched to pocket T's with my jeans and lightweight boots. Gwen was wearing a sleeveless blouse, short skirt, no pantyhose and sandals. Recently, at the office, she'd taken to wearing ties.

I'd overheard a colleague say, "I hate tie days."

"What's wrong with ties?" I'd never been tempted

to wear one, but on Gwen the skinny piece of silk fabric looked chic.

"Haven't you noticed? It's like she's PMS in a tie. Fashion of the super-bitch."

Lately, the tension between Gwen and me had little to do with work. Since my recent fright-night, we'd stopped making love. At bedtime she tucked herself in next to me and I cuddled her until she fell asleep. But I was withdrawn.

"Andrea," she'd said one morning when she woke up and found me staring at the ceiling. "Either talk about it or get over it."

"I am over it." I lay in bed, arms stiff at my sides.

"You're shutting me out."

I rolled toward her. "I'm trying to figure out how to amputate part of my psyche. You know, the part that used to be in love with someone else."

"You've never stopped loving her. You don't have to."

"When I've cauterized the wound, I'll let you know."

She'd taken a shower and slammed through her closet. "Shit. I need a new wardrobe." She'd put on a tie.

But while my colleagues suffered her frustration, she was patient with me. I mentioned it while we were preparing to leave for Mom's. "I know I've been a jerk. You're terrific."

"Surprised?" She picked up her purse. "How long did I have to wait for you to write decent copy?"

"Weeks. But that was work. This is —"

"This is hell." She dropped the car keys into my hand. "Let's go."

In my mother's entrance hall I caught Matt staring at Gwen's shaved legs, which were about a mile long. I gave him a ball-breaker glare and he slinked back. Everyone stared at Gwen's legs but if I had to beat someone up, I'd go for Matt.

Julia came to his rescue. "Matt, this is my sister, Andrea."

I relented and shook his hand. "Julia, Matt, I'd like you to meet Gwen Severence." Mom hurried to the door. "Gwen, my mother, Faye Fogelberg." Mom had taken back her maiden name.

They shook hands and Gwen handed Mom a bottle of wine.

She put on her reading glasses and examined the label. "Very nice. I've heard about this wine. It has an excellent bouquet."

I wanted to giggle. The bottle Gwen had brought was the brand featured in our wine-tasting ads. She put a steadying hand on my back. Mom's eyes flashed up, taking in the intimate gesture. Gwen had all the poise that I lacked. With her hand between my shoulder blades, her wine bottle in Mom's hands, I felt grown up.

Gwen murmured, "Thank you for having us."

Mom took the cue. "Dinner's almost ready. Julia, will you show our guests to the living room?"

As Mom turned away, I tugged on Gwen's hand. "Thanks."

She smiled. "What for?"

"You make it easier."

Mom called, "Andrea, will you give me a hand in here?"

"Pop quiz," Julia said. "I'll entertain Gwen."

In the kitchen, Mom was measuring balsamic

vinegar for salad dressing. *Coq au vin* was bubbling in the oven.

"Slice the French bread," she instructed. As I set to work with the bread knife, she said, "Gwen seems very nice."

"I'm glad you think so."

"How did you meet?"

"She's my boss."

"I see." Her voice pitched up a bit. "And you're —"

"Lovers, yeah. We spend most of our time at work, though."

"Then you consider this casual?"

I stopped slicing bread. I was only mildly stressed by Mom's interrogation but her assumption pissed me off. "There's nothing casual about my feelings for Gwen."

At that moment, Gwen walked in.

I shoved my fists into my pockets. I'd been planning to wait, to take my time until I'd released the rest of my grief. But my grieving process had a mind of its own and no intention of taking a holiday. Gwen had happened in spite of it. I'd been afraid that we were using each other, like guests at a funeral banquet making friends for the duration of the buffet. But if it had come down to being used, I would have opted for a six-pack and sent Gwen shopping for a new outfit a long time ago.

So I made my confession standing in Mom's kitchen, with Gwen in the doorway and me by the counter, crumbs from the French bread scattered like pigeon food around my boots. It may have been my proximity to Mom, too. Being close to her touched off my reckless streak.

I said to Gwen, "I'm glad you're here. I was just about to tell Mom that I love you."

Gwen strode to me and dropped a kiss on my forehead. She said, loud enough for Mom to hear, "The feeling's mutual." Then she whispered in my ear, "I love you, too."

I started to cry.

Julia came barging in, Matt at her heels. "I thought I smelled a family drama." Gwen put a protective arm around me and Julia noticed my tears. "Did you announce your engagement?"

Gwen murmured, "We'll talk later." She moved smoothly to my mother's side. "Faye, can I help you set the table?"

Mom put a stack of dishes in her hands and gave the wine and a corkscrew to Matt. He followed Gwen out, engrossed in the label.

Mom got a grip on her embarrassment. "We never discussed any of this when you were a teenager."

"I never had a relationship until college."

Julia handed me a tissue. "What just happened?"

Mom said, "Andrea's in love."

"Well, say congratulations."

"Oh, Andrea." Mom hugged me and after a minute the stiffness dissolved. "Mazel tov."

"Thanks." I blew my nose. It was nice to get some family support. Still, an unpleasant thought nagged me. When Gwen got her partnership, would she continue to share my bed? Would I be heartbroken by the end of the summer? I decided to keep a stiff upper lip, at least through dinner. "Mom, during dessert we'll discuss your sex life."

"A little respect for your elders, please."

Julia and I served the bread and salad. I made

sure there was ice water on the table. With a flourish, Mom dished up the chicken.

When everyone was seated, Julia said, "Gwen, tell us about yourself."

I said, "Hey. Mom invited us for dinner, not group therapy."

"Family meals are the best time for sharing," Matt said.

I spoke to Julia. "He's not human. He's an encounter group clone."

Gwen laughed. "I grew up with two brothers. Dinner conversation was usually secondary to getting a fair share of the food."

"Brothers, huh? Older or younger?"

"Both younger. James and Mark."

I said, "Uh-oh. Here comes eldest-sister bonding."

Matt smiled and nodded.

"What do they do?"

I forgave Julia her inquisition. She was asking the questions that I should have asked months ago. I'd resisted, as though knowledge of Gwen's family could send her away from me.

She said, "James is an architect. He lives in San Francisco."

"Is he gay?"

"Yes, good guess."

"Straight men use nicknames."

Matt looked relieved.

"How do your parents deal with having two gay kids?" Julia asked.

I glanced at Mom, who was making sure the wine glasses were full.

"Neither one of us has come out to our parents. They have their hands full with Mark. He has an obsessive-compulsive disorder and it's pretty severe. Dad and Mom remodeled their home to make an apartment for him. He can't work and he rarely leaves the house. It's a terrible, disabling illness."

Mom said, "How awful. It must be very hard on your parents."

"It is."

I hated myself. I hated that Julia, not me, had asked, and that the first I'd heard of Gwen's family was in my mother's home. I looked up and found Gwen's eyes on me. She smiled.

Matt was droning about treatments, some book or another.

Julia touched his hand. "What do you want to bet they know all that?" She said it gently and he shut up. My sister's social skills beat mine. She talked about psychiatric consumer politics.

Gwen confided to Mom that she was worried about her parents' retirement. "They should be traveling, not keeping watch over a grown son. James might move back to take some of the burden off. It would be a real sacrifice for him. He loves San Francisco."

"Would you go?" My voice sounded like it was coming out of a can.

She shook her head. "James is the caregiver, not me. I stayed with him while I was recuperating."

"I'd like to meet him."

I thought Julia would demand the details but she contented herself by saying, "Andrea has an obsessive-compulsive personality."

Gwen nodded. "Never misses a deadline."

Mom looked amused. I forgot that I was only drinking ice water and took a gulp of wine.

Gwen asked Julia, "What kind of work do you enjoy?"

Mom and I exchanged a look but Julia fielded the question. I'd been afraid that my family would rankle Gwen but the opposite seemed true. By some amazing chemistry, she had a calming effect on them.

"I should probably go back to school," Julia said, "but it takes so long and I'm tired of being sheltered." Her gaze landed on Mom. "I'm terrified that, whatever I do, I'll fall apart and end up back in the hospital." She looked at Gwen. "Got any advice?"

Gwen was thoughtful, sipping ice water. I noticed that she wasn't wearing lipstick. "Some people are lucky. They love doing something so much, they do it no matter what. They don't care about cocktail parties or retirement accounts. They just do what they love."

Mom, Julia and I were silent.

Matt said, "Cool."

"How do you find it?" Julia asked.

Gwen looked at me. "Sometimes it finds you."

"What do you love?"

Her eyes never left me. "I love to draw."

"Can I see your pictures?" I knew Julia didn't mean the advertisements. She meant the real stuff, Gwen's art. She was brazen; I hadn't had the guts to ask.

"All my paintings are with James, in San Francisco. I have photos, though, if you'd like to see those."

"I'll call you."

Mom began to clear the table. Reluctantly, I got up to help.

In the kitchen, Mom said, "Gwen is a very special person."

I muttered, "If Julia turns bi, I'll kill her." Mom distracted me by putting a cake into my hands. It had candles on it. "What's this?"

"In honor of your birthday."

"That was last month."

"We have some catching up to do."

"You shouldn't have."

"Humor me." She lit the candles, took the cake and carried it into the dining room. Everyone sang. I blushed. Julia gave me a card. Mom gave me a watch.

I slipped off my old one and admired the new one. "Thanks. It's great."

Julia said, "I had to help her pick it out. Mom doesn't get butch at all."

Gwen asked, "How old are you?"

"Twenty-four, last month. How old are you?"

"Thirty-five."

It was a relief to get the basics out of the way.

"Happy birthday." She gave me a kiss. It didn't even bother me that Mom was watching.

On the drive home, Gwen found a rock station and turned up the volume. "Do you like to dance?"

"I'm a klutz."

"Julia's terrific. You don't mind about us getting together, do you?"

"Of course not," I lied. I admitted, "I thought you'd hate my family. Now I'm afraid you'll fall in love with my sister."

She ran a finger along my thigh. "That position's taken."

I turned down the music. "Are you going to dump me when you get the partnership?"

"Can we take this one day at a time?"

"Is that your way of saying yes?"

"You'll turn anything into a crisis." She turned up the music again. "I hope we can keep working together."

"I can't believe I'm falling in love with such a bitch."

I had to strain to hear her over the music. "I love how we are together. The writing and the art. At work. At home. I just can't do it all at once, okay?"

My shoulders had begun to ache and I made an effort to loosen my grip on the steering wheel. I kept my eyes on the road, half-blinded by oncoming headlights. It took forever to get home.

Chapter 17

My pages of looseleaf writing were piling up, filled with images of Gwen. It was a relief, on Sunday afternoon, to write words that no one else was going to read, words without graphics, not even Gwen's drawings. I wrote not to inform, merely to describe; to satiate myself, not to sell.

It was a warm day and I had my window open. Summer was the only season that Ryan and I hadn't shared. We'd had Christmas but not summer vacation. A breeze rustled my pages and I began writing a story about a bitter man who kills himself, only to find that he hates death more than life.

His immortal soul swooped like a great bird, preying on living thoughts. Mourners kept their heads bowed, all the while dwelling on shoe polish, stiff necks, the Saturday night supper to be shopped for and prepared. Someone was fretting about Junior's soccer game — missed for a funeral. The office secretary kept reminding herself that the car needed gas, the cat needed litter.

In the midst of the mundane, there was a note of grief, a footnote, really.

"Too bad about Chuck. Who knew the guy was on the edge?"

The preacher was droning.

"Cut to the chase, why doesn't he? If Chuck's in heaven, good for him. If not, well, some things are better left unknown."

But he could tell them. He'd pick on someone, maybe the secretary. He had enough strength to bleed into her life, to give her a nightmare, a string of bad luck. Eventually, a car accident. He sat on his coffin, cross-legged like a swami. There was nothing, he vowed as they lowered his remains into the ground, as useless as a mourner who didn't mean it.

With the story half-done, I shoved the pages back into the folder. I didn't like where it was headed. I'd meant to write about remorse, not revenge. I moved to the window and rested my hip on the sill. It hadn't occurred to me that Ryan, if she still had consciousness, might also be grieving. And if so, was she ready to let me go? Perhaps, selfishly, I was holding her back, calling her out of the lake time and again when all she sought was the peace in the silver depths. The last thing I wanted to do was torment her.

I opened a beer and prowled my apartment, looking for a distraction. I ended up back at the window, still dwelling on Ryan. Like a penny from the gutter, I picked up the old argument, turning it this way and that.

"I wanted to believe you about endless love," I whispered. "But I can't spend the rest of my life in love with a dead jock."

I drained my beer. I was tired, so tired of the grief. And I was really sick of spending Sunday afternoons alone.

The following weekend, Julia came over. It was Friday night and she'd arranged for Dad to bring her to my apartment. He was in town for a vitamin conference. He tooted, waved his arm out the window and drove away.

"I can't believe Mom let him drive you."

"They're starting to call each other Faye and Sam."

"First names? What's the deal?"

"Dad wants to chip in for my rent when I get my own place."

"Julia —"

"I'm advocating for myself."

"You're priming them for a fight."

"Dad has a right to support me if he wants to."

She dropped her overnight bag on my couch. Mom

was probably doing extra therapy sessions, but Julia was spending the night.

"Mom did the grunt work while Dad screwed around. Now the hard part's over and he wants back in."

"Who says the hard part's over? And what do you care who pays my rent? I'm not asking you."

"Maybe you should," I yelled. "I didn't see you for years, either. Why don't you let me buy you back?"

Because of my raised voice, I didn't hear the knock on my door. Julia flounced to open it and Gwen came in carrying a photo album.

"Am I interrupting?"

I said, "Only a sibling spat. Come in and take sides."

"Do you mind if I sit this one out?"

"Did you notice," Julia asked, "that you're on Mom's side and I'm on Dad's?"

"You're running the family. What else is new?"

"It always used to be the other way around. You took Dad and I got Mom. We've switched."

"I'm so ticked at Dad I barely said two words to him."

"But you're fighting with me."

"He practically abandoned you."

"It's not your fight. It's not our fight."

I hated it that she was being reasonable. "It pisses me off," I snapped.

Gwen asked, "Anyone want coffee?"

"Decaf," Julia said.

Gwen went into the kitchen.

The more I thought about Dad, the more upset I got. "He needs to cut his hair and get a job."

"God, Andrea. You sound like Mom."

"Shit. How'd that happen?"

Gwen poked her head out, held up a canister. "Honey? Is this decaf?"

I took over in the kitchen. I served coffee and a plate of cookies.

Julia said, "Keep her. She makes a good wife."

"I can fix my own plumbing."

"Useful," Gwen agreed.

They sat on the couch, heads together. I perched on the armrest and peered over Gwen's shoulder, looking at the photos I hadn't known existed until Julia had asked. My sister was like an archaeologist, unearthing relationships. I wondered what kind of family would finally get pieced together. Gwen rested a hand on my leg while Julia turned the album pages.

Gwen's paintings covered huge canvases, full of bold hues and vivid, abstract designs. Julia studied them silently. On my leg, Gwen's hand tightened. Toward the back of the album, the pictures were smaller, more concrete — landscapes viewed from a long way off, full of detail but far away.

"I did those when I was in San Francisco."

"They're beautiful." Julia touched the page. "Almost like you're looking down, like an overhead view."

"Yes. That's the effect I wanted."

I caressed her shoulders. When she looked up, I gave her a lingering kiss.

Julia said, "Kinky."

Gwen smiled. "If I'd known this was going to turn you on, I'd have brought a paint set over weeks ago."

"She's blushing," Julia observed. "She's a prude."

Gwen laughed. "You'd be surprised."

Julia held up a hand. "We're not sharing."

"Glass of water, anyone?" I retreated to the kitchen.

When I came back, Julia was asking, "Do you have a studio?"

"My place is too small. I was thinking about moving into a two-bedroom."

"What do you think about when you paint?" Julia was turning pages again.

"I used to fill every corner of a canvas. I love the force of the paint."

Julia was examining a photo. "I like your colors. Most people think gold and red stand for wealth and power. But I interpret them as beauty and strength."

"Did you study art?"

"If they gave credit for art therapy in psychiatric hospitals, I'd have a master's degree." She tapped a picture. "What about the little ones?"

"I guess I was thinking about life."

"Life from a distance. You should get back in touch with the red. It makes you come alive."

"You're a good critic."

While they talked, I called out for pizza. We devoured gooey slices, staying up late and listening to music. At two a.m. I clicked on the TV and found a poorly dubbed movie about a giant robot, one of my childhood favorites. Gwen was drinking diet soda; Julia's was caffeine-free. I was the only one drinking the real stuff and I was wide awake.

Gwen took a closer look at the screen. "You're not serious."

"This is really cool."

Julia said, "You're regressing. I'm going to bed."

She looked tired and I felt a twinge of guilt for keeping the party going so late. I said, "I put clean sheets on. Help yourself." I turned to Gwen. "You're welcome to stay but I'm sleeping on the couch."

"What are you doing tomorrow? And don't even think about coming to work."

"Do you want to hang out with us?"

"Yes, but not before noon."

"You're working?"

"Sleeping, I hope. Not on your couch, though."

I sighed. "Let's go to the Fine Arts museum." She kissed my nose. "Get lost, Gwen. I have a date with the giant robot." The monster was shooting missiles out of his knuckles.

She said, "I have no idea what makes this relationship work."

I got up and walked her to the door. "You're beautiful and strong. I knew it before I saw your paintings."

"Get some sleep."

When she had gone, I looked in on Julia. "Hey, sis?" She mumbled something I didn't hear. "What?"

"I'm tired. Go to sleep."

I dragged a blanket and pillow back to the couch. I wasn't sleepy so I turned the TV volume very low. When I eventually nodded off the good guys were winning, but with a show like *Giant Robot*, that was predictable.

On Saturday, Gwen left her car at my place and we rode the subway to the museum. Julia and Gwen checked their guidebooks and headed for contemporary art. I stuffed my tour map in my pocket and wandered through the historical exhibits, examining Japanese daggers and Egyptian tombs. Eventually, I found myself in the wing that housed European paintings. Several long rooms were given over to religious themes.

I stepped closer, trying to make sense of the halos and luminous eyes. In portrait after portrait, saints gazed heavenward. I rocked onto the balls of my feet, trying to decipher the pious expressions. No one looked happy. Faces were pleading, questioning, more often anguished. Finally, one painting arrested me and I studied it.

The woman kneeling before the cross also gazed into heaven, but there was something in her face that I hadn't seen in the other pictures. Beneath the suffering, in the way that sunlight sometimes escapes around the edges of clouds, I could make out hope. When I stood back, hope and suffering blended until I was no longer looking at pain, but ecstasy. I was still staring at the painting when Gwen and Julia found me.

"There you are. Julia said you'd be in here." Gwen put her arm around me. "I didn't know you went for Christian art."

"I'm just looking around." I pulled the crumpled map out of my pocket. "I got lost."

Julia said, "Her dead girlfriend wanted to be a priest."

I kept studying the museum map, trying to figure out how I'd meandered from Egypt to Europe.

Gwen released me. "Do you want to be alone?"

I shook my head. "Let's get out of here."

I was afraid Julia might try to do art therapy but she was silent.

We took the subway to Chinatown, the train

lurching at each stop. Julia seemed glazed. Gwen was quiet and I didn't try to make conversation.

At the restaurant, I sat across from Gwen and stared at her throughout the meal. I'd been trying to recapture a feeling but love didn't work that way. It didn't repeat.

Gwen made small talk and Julia seemed to revive a bit. Every now and then she said something I couldn't quite follow. Gwen glanced at me but I shrugged. I had too much on my mind to stay with the conversation.

On the train ride home, I stood close to Gwen. I wanted to touch her, smell her, taste her. I wanted her.

At six-thirty, Mom arrived to drive Julia home.

I opened the door. "Hi. Want some leftovers? We had Chinese."

"I was going to invite everyone to dinner."

I called, "Anyone hungry?"

Gwen and Julia came out of my bedroom. Julia was clutching her ponytail. "Gwen knows a neat way to do a French braid."

Gwen said to Julia, "Let your hair grow. It's pretty. Hi, Faye."

Mom inspected the handiwork. "Why don't you wear yours long, Gwen? I'd go back to long hair if mine was as thick and gorgeous as yours."

I said, "Mom, you've always had short hair. You said long hair was too hot for tennis."

"Well, Andrea, I wasn't always a tennis Mom. Julia didn't start lessons until she was eight. Before that, I hadn't played since college."

Gwen asked, "How old were you when you got married?"

"Twenty-four. A lifetime ago."

"My age," I murmured.

I took the leftovers out of the fridge. Before I could offer to reheat anything, Mom opened a carton.

"Mmm. Ginger chicken. Forks?"

I handed her one and she began eating out of the container. She finished the chicken and began on the next carton while Gwen told her about the art exhibits. I leaned against the counter, listening to Gwen, watching Mom eat. I moved closer to Gwen, until I was practically on top of her.

Finally, Mom looked at Julia. She said, "I'll take you home, honey." I heard a note of concern.

Gwen took a long time being polite, saying what a nice day she had and how she wanted to get together again. When the door closed, she asked, "Want to see if there's any monster robot movies on TV?"

I pushed her to the couch, made her sit down and straddled her lap. "I'm going to show you how much I want you." I skinned off my shirt.

Before her lips found my breast, she murmured, "About time."

I kept opening my eyes, searching her expression. She caught me watching and smiled. Embarrassed, I began to go down, to love her but also to hide.

She held my shoulders. "Stay here." She cupped my face. "What are you looking for?"

When I looked at her I saw love and hope, and a little pain. But the emotions hadn't blended yet, or maybe I hadn't found the right perspective. "I want to love you," I whispered, then lay back down in her arms.

* * * * *

We were still in bed on Sunday morning when the phone rang. Mom's voice said, "Andrea?"

"Mom? What's wrong?"

Beside me, Gwen sat up.

"I'm at the hospital. With Julia."

"Oh, Jesus. Is she okay?"

"Yes, but it's a setback."

"I'm on my way. Does Dad know?"

"He's at a conference. I called his pager."

Gwen was already pulling on clothes while Mom gave me directions. I hung up the phone. "Jesus," I said. "Not again."

"Andrea?" Gwen's eyes looked huge.

"Julia's in the hospital. Mom didn't get into the details. I hope to God she didn't cut herself."

Gwen drove, keeping the speedometer steady on eighty-five. There was no traffic. The emergency waiting area was full of hard plastic chairs. On a TV screen, a televangelist frothed silently. I gave Mom a hug, then Gwen did.

"How is she?" Gwen asked.

"Stable," Mom said. "The attending psychiatrist wants to admit her and evaluate her medication."

The sliding doors parted and Dad walked in. He still had his ponytail but he was dressed in a suit and tie. Mom was wearing a crumpled sweat outfit. Gwen and I were in jeans and T-shirts.

"Faye?"

"Talk to the doctor, Sam. She's been trying to do too much too fast. And she was fatigued from her sleepover. It's no wonder her levels are fluctuating."

"Cutting?"

"She nicked a superficial vein on her inner thigh."

"Is she lucid now?"

"It comes and goes. She asked me to bring her in this morning. She wants to be admitted." Mom's voice shook. "I should have seen this coming on. I'm sorry, Sam." Dad had a cell phone out and Mom fought to regain her composure. "I already have a call in to Dr. Meadows."

I'd heard the name. Julia's psychiatrist.

"She'll be fine." Dad sounded confident. "Once they get the medication adjusted, you'll be able to take her home."

"She was fatigued," Mom said again.

I wanted to keep standing, to stay with the conversation, but my legs wouldn't cooperate. I folded myself into a plastic chair. Fatigue. Sleepovers. Too much too soon. How much of what had happened to Julia was my fault? It was the same old story. I was irresponsible, thinking of no one but myself. I'd wanted to have a party, get her a place to live and teach her to drive. Anything to be a part of her life. *At whose expense?* Mom was right. I was family strain that Julia didn't need.

I felt a hand on my shoulder and looked up to see Dad standing over me. He spoke in a low voice. "Take it easy, kid. It's nothing your Mom and I can't handle." He began to turn away and almost bumped into Gwen. He stuck out his hand. "Sam Stern, Andrea's Dad."

"Gwen Severence." She shook his hand. "If there's anything Andrea and I can do —"

"We've got it covered."

Dad went off to tangle with the doctors and admissions staff and to make more phone calls. He would reach Julia's doctor. Medication levels would be seen to and Julia would be fine. Just like Dad said.

Mom would take Julia home. Just like before. But I wasn't part of the equation. I doubted that Julia would be visiting with me again anytime soon. Gwen sat beside me and I welcomed her comforting arm.

Mom appeared in front of me. "Andrea, please believe me when I say this isn't your fault. Julia and I have been arguing. She told me that you took her to look at apartments."

"Single rooms only," I muttered. "I wouldn't have let her live in any of those places. Not in a million years."

Mom sat down. I was sandwiched between her and Gwen. She said, "The medication isn't perfect. Julia has to deal with psychotic episodes. It's something we all have to learn to accept." She put a hand on my arm. "She needs stability. She also needs her sister."

I didn't want to cry on Mom, so I turned and put my head on Gwen's shoulder. Mom handed me a tissue, though.

By the time Dad came back, a new preacher had commandeered the TV screen. I found myself thinking that the tele-pastor would look better with long hair. The preacher needed a ponytail.

Dad said, "Dr. Meadows called in new orders. She'll be over first thing in the morning. We'll have to give it a few days."

"I'll go in to see her," Mom said. She turned to me. "I'm sorry you had to drive all this way, Andrea."

I said, "I'll call later to see how she's doing." I didn't press about a visitor's pass. Not while Mom was still being polite.

Dad said, "I'm glad you called, Faye." He bent to

kiss my cheek. "I'll see you later. Ms. Severence," he smiled at Gwen. "I'm sure I'll see you, too." His business completed, Dad left.

Before Mom turned away, Gwen stepped forward. "Do you need groceries, Faye? We'd be happy to go to the market."

I almost smiled, thinking of the time I'd brought groceries for Gwen, when she'd had the flu. She was a quick study in the mores of my family. Mom hesitated.

I said, "Good idea. Do you still leave a key by the back door?"

"Under the begonia pot. If you're sure it's not an inconvenience."

Gwen and I went shopping. I'd forgotten my wallet. Gwen paid for the groceries. When we dropped them off, Mom wasn't back yet. I set up a pot of decaf for her. All she had to do was turn it on to brew.

On the way home, I said, "Thanks, Gwen."

"I hope Julia's okay."

We didn't say much else. When we got back to my place, Dad was parked out front.

"Do you want me to stick around?" Gwen asked.

I shook my head, then changed my mind. "No. Yes. You don't have to," I said lamely. She waited for me to decide. "I'd better deal with Dad. I'll call you later."

She kissed my cheek. As she drove away, I had a sudden urge to run after her. I pressed my heels into the cement. Dad climbed out of his car. He was driving a Nissan. One of the nicer models.

He asked, "Have you eaten anything today?"

I looked at my wrist. I'd forgotten my watch, too.

In my pocket I had change, a couple of subway tokens and my keys. That was it.

Dad said, "It's past lunchtime. Let's go to the North End. My treat."

"I thought you had a conference or something."

"We got most of our business done yesterday. What a bunch of sprout-heads. How about some carbonara?"

"I thought you liked that organic stuff."

"We're all entitled to a mistake." I'd never heard Dad admit to one. He held the car door for me. "I'm giving legal counsel to one of the health food chains. Drug companies are lobbying to keep natural remedies off the shelves. We believe consumers have a right to alternative treatments."

"I bet you and Julia have a lot to talk about."

"We're finding some common ground."

While we were driving, I asked, "Is she going to be okay?" Why did children insist that parents answer impossible questions? But I wanted his reassurance.

"She knows how to cope with her illness better than any of us. Part of her adjustment to being home is letting us know how we can help."

"When Mom gets over the shock and comes to her senses, she's not going to let me see her."

"The time is past when this family can split itself down the middle. We have to find a way to get along."

It took me a minute to figure out why he sounded different. He wasn't using his courtroom voice. It really sounded like Dad.

He parked in a North End garage whose tourist rates made me wince. The restaurant he picked looked like it belonged in an Italian piazza. Windows folded back to give it the feel of a street café. I peered around, half-expecting to see sculpture and fountains. We were seated at one of the open-air tables.

"Wine?" he asked.

"Coffee." He ordered me a cappuccino. "You don't have to be extravagant," I said.

"Can't I treat my daughter to lunch?"

"I appreciate what you did for Julia. You don't owe me anything, Dad. You don't have to prove that you love me, too."

He studied me over the top of his menu. "You used to be an optimistic child. When did you get cynical?"

"When I realized my parents were fighting their battles through me and my sister."

"I'm glad to hear you've been talking to Julia. So have I." A waiter came over. "Are you hungry?"

"Not really."

He ordered a fried artichoke appetizer, cioppino and a bottle of Chianti. I ordered soup. He told the waiter to pour wine for me as well.

He raised his glass. *"L'Chaim."*

"L'Chaim," I answered. To life. I took a sip and silently added the rest. *To love.*

"How's work?" He put a couple of artichoke hearts on my bread plate.

"It's good."

"And your relationship?"

"I wish you could have met Gwen under better circumstances."

"Faye thinks highly of her. I'm afraid we've both had to wrestle with our homophobia."

"At long last. Parental approval." I speared an artichoke.

"I've always accepted you, Andrea."

I thought about it. "You never gave me a hard time, but I'm not sure if that was acceptance or neglect."

"Some of each."

"When did it dawn on you that you might be homophobic?"

"I made a pass at a lesbian."

"Oh, please."

"What can I say? She was wearing a dress."

"And you think anything with nice legs is fair game? If you go near Gwen, I'll break your knees. By the way, that doesn't make you a homophobe. It means you're a prick."

"That's what Julia said. Among other things." He poured more wine. His cioppino had arrived, swimming with every kind of shellfish. I leaned over and scooped out some of the good stuff. He pushed the dish closer. "Try some calamari."

I ate clams and squid off his plate, bread soaked in olive oil, and drank another glass of Chianti. I couldn't believe it was Sunday afternoon and I was getting soused with Dad. I felt guilty, thinking about Mom and Julia. What right did Dad and I have to be imbibing when my whole family was in crisis. Then again, my family was always in crisis. And Julia and Mom had plenty of groceries, thanks to Gwen.

I asked, "What else did Julia say?"

He put down his fork, picked up his wineglass. "She said my marriage was over a long time ago and it was time to let go of the animosity. She called me a self-absorbed jerk who always put myself before my family. Except on vacation. I think I deserve a little credit for some good family vacations."

"Enough with the editorializing."

"And she made a lot of noise about parents owing it to their children to get along."

"That's a nice sentiment but we're all grown up now."

"Julia had her first schizophrenic break during the time that Faye and I were fighting a lot. She needs to see us making an effort. If you girls marry, have children, we'll both be at the wedding, or . . . well, you know the point I'm trying to make."

I tried to picture a Jewish-Italian wedding, Gwen's relatives and mine mixing Chianti and Manischewitz. Thinking about weddings made me remember something else he'd said. "How come you told me that you and Mom were never in love?"

"I lied. Andrea, once upon a time, your parents loved each other. I'm sorry it didn't last."

"You're such a jerk, Dad." I ate more of his artichokes.

By the time we stumbled out of the restaurant, we were both too drunk to drive.

I fished in my pocket for subway fare. "Come on. You can crash at my place."

"I don't want to put you out."

"One family member in the hospital is enough for today. You get the couch. It's going to cost you a fortune to get your car back tomorrow."

At home, I called Gwen. "Dad's sleeping over. We had a little too much wine."

She said, "Don't be late for work in the morning."

I called Mom. "Everything okay?"

"When I left, Julia was resting." I thought that sounded like a euphemism for spaced-out. She said, "Please tell Gwen I said thank you."

On Monday morning I drove back to the North End and Dad ransomed his Nissan. We double-parked in the street and got out to say goodbye. I was showered and ready for work. He'd left his tie off. I was yawning.

"Let me buy you some coffee."

"I'll get some at work."

"I insist." He dashed into a café and came out with double lattés.

"Thanks."

"I'm proud of you, Andrea."

"You, too, Dad."

He honked and drove off.

Chapter 18

Julia was in the hospital for five days. When she got home, Gwen and I went to visit at Mom's. No one felt like cooking so we sent out to the local taco joint. It was a subdued get-together. Julia's schizophrenia wasn't going to go away, but I hadn't been banished, either. Julia would stay with Mom. She wasn't hinting about getting her own apartment. And Mom seemed to have crossed a threshold, finally able to admit that there were other people in the family — me, Dad, and now Gwen.

In Mom's living room, I sat next to Gwen and

nibbled nacho chips. Mom didn't even seem worried about crumbs. No one was talking about jobs or training or careers. I noticed a couple of arts and crafts projects that Julia had brought home from the support center. Gwen and Julia talked about a movie they wanted to see. Mom said that the folks in her parents' group had been understanding.

I leaned close to Julia. "Does your leg hurt?"

"Not really." Her eyes darted guiltily to Mom. "This wasn't the first time."

I saw Gwen glance at Mom.

"She was hiding it," Mom said. She was sitting casually on the sofa. The stiffness that I usually saw in her demeanor hadn't materialized.

Julia said, "It's cleansing. Like I'm getting the poison out. Like they do with leeches."

I wanted to yell at Mom, *This is what you get for acting like a girl and shaving your legs. Throw away the razors.* Of course, Gwen shaved her legs. There were razors at my place, too.

"When I'm psychotic, I believe it," Julia said.

Mom said, "Dr. Meadows wants us to try a few sessions with a family counselor. I need to relax my . . . parenting style."

Within a matter of weeks, I'd heard both of my parents attesting to self-assessment. I said, "I think Dad quit vitamins."

"He's still selling on the side," Mom said. "He gave me a good deal on calcium supplements. Are you taking calcium, Andrea? You should. Your grandmother had osteoporosis."

"Okay, Mom." I tried a few more nacho chips.

After our visit, Gwen drove me home and put me to bed.

"My family's nuts," I said.

She nuzzled against me. "Now I know where you get it from."

As August got hotter, anyone who wasn't on vacation was waiting to take a turn. The senior partner had announced his retirement, effective Labor Day, but no plans for reorganization were forthcoming. Gwen spent a lot of time upstairs.

On the Friday before Labor Day, I couldn't bear it any longer. Either Gwen was going to get her partnership and break up with me, or she'd find another agency, leave town and break up with me. When everyone had gone home, I walked into her office.

She said, "Hi, cute girl. Got any plans for the weekend?"

"I need a break. I want to take next week off."

She sat back. "Is your desk clear?"

"I'll come in tomorrow and get caught up."

She regarded me but didn't ask for an invitation. I held my tongue. If we went away together, nothing would change. She'd still be waiting for me to get over Ryan, and I'd be waiting for her to leave. It was a juvenile instinct, but I wanted to get out of town first. "Going anywhere special?"

"I've never seen the coast of Maine."

"I've heard Camden's pretty."

"Maybe I'll check it out."

"I'll give Julia a call. There's a new film series in Cambridge."

"She'd like that." I leaned over her desk and gave her a peck on the cheek. "See you when I get back?" I hadn't meant it to be a question.

"Make sure your butt's in your chair a week from Monday."

"You, too," I said.

On Saturday I worked the whole day, tying up every loose end I could find. Gwen didn't come in. Saturday night I cleaned my apartment, including the inside of my refrigerator. I ditched leftovers, washed Tupperware and hauled out the trash. Then I threw jeans and T-shirts into an overnight bag. Early on Sunday morning I made a Thermos of coffee, gassed the car and headed north.

A map of coastal Maine lay unfolded on my passenger seat but I ignored it. As soon as I reached the city limit, I knew where I was going. I followed the interstate into New Hampshire and took the exit for Durham University.

The college town was quiet. The air felt cooler than in Boston, but fall hadn't officially arrived, and the few students I saw were wearing summer shorts. I circled the campus then drove to the outskirts, parked and got out. On Christmas, the wooded path where Ryan and I walked had been snow-dusted, awash in moonlight. Now, in summer daylight, it was ordinary brown and green. Soon dozens of students would be tramping on it, hurrying past the field where Ryan had pulled me to her, our jeans soaked, her breath warm, my throat wrapped in her gift, the cashmere scarf.

From where I stood, the field was around a bend but I didn't bother to walk to it. Whatever magic had possessed it that night was gone. I was here as a visitor in the wrong season. To say goodbye, I'd come to the wrong place.

I got back in my car and drove inland, toward the lake, arriving in town as the church services were letting out. I waited for the traffic to clear, then took the road to Ryan's chapel. The church doors were still open so I sat in my car. Finally, a gray-haired man wearing a priest's collar locked up and drove away. I got out and stretched. Trees were in full leaf with no hint yet of red or yellow. The front lawn looked well-tended and someone had already planted a row of white chrysanthemums. If they were hearty enough, they'd last through October.

Slowly, I walked to the cemetery. It was smaller than I remembered, and prettier. Without the black-clad, muddy-shoed funeral crowd, the grassy plots looked peaceful, the grave-markers clean. I had no trouble recalling the exact location of Ryan's grave and I was almost upon it when I realized I wasn't alone. A woman was coming toward me from the far side of the church. She must have come out of a back door; I hadn't seen another car, had been certain of my solitude. I stopped to let her walk past but she also stood still.

After a moment, she said, "Andrea?"

Mrs. Mann and I reached the grave at the same moment.

My first thought was to apologize. "I'm sorry. I thought everyone was gone."

She smiled warmly. "Ben took Brittany to a soccer game. He'll come back for me in a while. I like to have a quiet visit with Ryan now and then." She looked at me kindly. "Is that why you're here?"

I was flooded with guilt. I should have come sooner. I'd stayed away too long. "I, um, didn't plan — I'm sorry," I faltered. "I'll come back another time."

"Don't be silly. I'm glad you're here."

Her navy dress had pockets and a simple neckline. I stared at her plain silver cross, remembering Ryan's Celtic pendant. Mrs. Mann showed none of the nervousness of our previous visit. When I'd been in her home, she'd poured the tea with a trembling hand. Now she looked relaxed, comfortable even, at her daughter's graveside. She came to stand next to me and linked her arm through mine. After a moment, we clasped hands. Hers was large and strong, like Ryan's had been. I felt the calluses on her palm and wondered if she'd been the one to dig the flower beds. Chrysanthemums bordered the gravestone, set flush with the ground. I let go of her hand and dropped to my knees.

The stone said, *Shelly Ryan Mann,* and gave the dates, which spanned twenty years.

"I didn't know her first name was Shelly."

Mrs. Mann crouched beside me, sitting easily on her heels. Definitely a gardener. "She never liked her given name. My maiden name is Ryan, and from the time she was five, that was the only name she'd answer to." She smiled. "When she knew what she wanted, nothing could dissuade her."

I ran my fingers over the letters. The stone also bore two engraved emblems. In one corner, I

249

recognized the cross in the circle. My hand moved to touch it. In the other corner, my fingers traced four curving lines. Tile had been inlaid, set into the granite so that each graceful line was a different color.

"We learned about the rainbow flag at our parents' group. It seemed . . . appropriate." She touched the stone. "We each chose a color. Green for me, for my Irish roots, I suppose. Brittany wanted purple and Ben chose red. And blue was always Ryan's favorite."

Around the stripe of blue tile, the granite shone dark gray. When the sun hit it, burnished flecks of silver stood out.

"It's perfect."

I stood up and reached to help Mrs. Mann. She rose smoothly and we stood in silence, our heads bowed.

Ironically, my thoughts, which never gave me a moment's peace, were quiet, as still as the stone markers dotting the graves. I was aware of a breeze rustling the leaves, and a pair of squirrels chasing each other when they should have been hunting stores for hibernation. I raised my head, not distracted, just more comfortable looking out, rather than down. I inhaled the sweet air and let my shoulders relax. My feet stayed planted at the edge of Ryan's resting place.

Except she wasn't there. The grave was only a symbol, a plot of earth given over to her memory, the engraved stone a reminder, a dedication to our love for her. It was as good a place as any to give up her body, the cemetery like a meditation garden, a place to focus the mind in prayer. Perhaps Mrs. Mann was praying for peace, for the safekeeping of her daughter's soul. No words came into my mind.

Ryan, what do I pray for? What do we do now?

I listened to the stirring trees. How welcome would my thoughts be if they reached her? Perhaps she'd feel them like a sliver picked up from a wooden gate, a slim reminder of human existence. In my grief, I'd thought of her only as she'd been in the flesh. But perhaps her spirit was in the trees, or the clouds that gathered over the lake, the rain that pelted down. Maybe her love was in the soft ripples on the water. I thought about the dreams I'd refused to believe, the glowing presence that was undeniably . . . Ryan. If a soul could step through the veil, surely hers had done so.

Faith entered my consciousness like a pinprick. Skepticism crowded in, but briefly — the sky expanded. The clouds spread apart and sun and wind beat through the opening. For a split second, I understood why people gazed heavenward.

I blinked and found Mrs. Mann watching me. She reached into her pocket and pulled out a necklace. I knew at once that it was Ryan's cross.

"I always bring it to church. In my pocket, it feels like she's sitting next to me." She paused. "Andrea, I'd like you to have it."

I shook my head. It was a minute before I could speak. "No. I can't."

"I won't pretend it's not difficult to part with. We all hold onto different things, don't we? Even when it's time to pack up a child's belongings, how do you begin to put them away?" She smiled, but her eyes were sad. "Sometimes we hold onto too much, and for too long. Ryan's been trying to tell me that, but

I'm afraid I haven't been listening very well. I believe she wants to help both of us." I stared at her. I'd just begun to accept the possibility of spirits. Mrs. Mann apparently had regular conversations with them. She held out the cross. "Ryan wants you to have this. I'm certain of it."

I couldn't make myself reach for it. "Why?"

She looked up, over my head. "I suspect you're beginning to find your own answer to that. Go on, dear. Please take it, if only to bolster my faith that I'm doing the right thing."

Our fingers touched. My hands, normally so awkward with jewelry, worked the clasp easily. My hesitation vanished and I hung it around my neck. It lay just below my throat.

"Well, it makes sense now," she said. "Seeing it on you makes me remember how it looked on her, when she was so full of life. That's how she wants to be remembered." Her face and voice were full of peace. I heard tires crunching. "There's Ben." She looked at me a moment longer. "It'll be okay, now. I know it will." She kissed my cheek. "It was nice seeing you again, Andrea. Goodbye." She hurried around the church to meet her husband.

I sat on the grass, then lay down on my back, enjoying the sun and the country smells. I dozed. When I awoke and looked up, I felt the pinprick again. This time I didn't chase it away. It was a feeling I didn't understand, an inkling of faith that Ryan still existed, although beyond my reach. There was a peacefulness, too, an inner restfulness when I thought of her. And underneath, swelling to the surface, a feeling that was something like awe. I closed my eyes and let it fill me.

Chapter 19

I tried numerous roadside motels before I found a vacancy, then paid too much for a drab room with a lifeless TV. But it was a holiday weekend and I was lucky to get anything, especially since I was traveling without having called ahead. I slept soundly, and on Monday I made my way to Maine.

Following the Maine coast was like tracing a line on a piece of crinkled paper, with the pen bouncing down as well as up. I bypassed the outlet malls, then drove by shipyards and working ports. Each town center hosted a steeple, thrift store, shoe shop and eatery. Shingled roofs were steeply pitched to fend off hard-driving blizzards. Tantalizing glimpses of ocean pulled me along.

The drive took longer because I kept pulling off the road to watch the ocean. The water sparkled, sun-tipped and white-capped, frothing on the rocky shore. In Camden's protected cove, sailboats bobbed, safe from the sea swells. On the broad avenues, grand homes vied for bed-and-breakfast guests. I found an inn on Main Street and asked for a room.

The innkeeper took in my jeans, windblown hair and three-season windbreaker. I pushed up my sleeve and pretended to check the time. Mom's watch was the most expensive thing I was wearing.

"No reservation?" I felt like a schoolgirl caught without homework. "It's foliage season, mind you."

I checked my watch again to be sure of the date. "Today's Labor Day."

"Where're you from?"

"Boston."

She grunted. "Peak season depends on the weather. It can turn anytime," she warned. "How long will you be staying?"

"I'd like a room for the week."

She tapped at a computerized register. "Through Wednesday night, Thursday check-out. We're booked after that."

Gratefully, I watched her log the reservation. I didn't know what I was going to do in Camden for three days, but it was better than trying to negotiate night by night. If one tree got cranky and turned orange, I'd be paying double.

My sleeping quarters had a view of the street, an easy chair and a small writing desk. I left my unpacked bag on the bed. Outside, I walked the length of a wooden porch and peered down on the mill river. An old-fashioned waterwheel was scenic enough to compete with the impending foliage. I pocketed my room key and went into town.

The harbor wasn't hard to find, bristling as it was with sailboat masts. The afternoon was mellowly warm, and I walked along the water and up the merchant-lined street. Posters in shop windows advertised folk music on Saturdays and a farmers' market. I'd be gone before the entertainment arrived. I turned my attention to an art gallery's schooner display, then dawdled in a used-book store. Edna St. Vincent Millay had lived in the region, a fact I learned when I questioned the price tag on a slim volume of her poetry. I dug out my wallet, determined to have a good time.

I drank coffee in a café adorned with local art, then flirted with the waitress until she told me it was her art on the walls. With a pang, I thought of Gwen.

"Nice style," I said, and moved on.

At the pub, I made the best of thick chowder and locally brewed beer. After a while I stopped eating and kept drinking. In a corner booth, I drank until I couldn't stand and then sat until I was fairly sure I could find my room again. Sometime after the beer and during the mulling, I concluded that I'd never been one to do things by halves. In school, I'd followed up every point. In the kitchen, I left the skin on the chicken. Recently, I'd been thinking about polishing a few short stories and priming my mailbox for the rejection notes. With my elbows propped on either side of an empty glass, I reminded myself that

I hated to let go of an argument. And I didn't want to let go of Gwen.

"So keep her," I mumbled. I sat up as straight as my drunken stupor would allow.

Ryan's love had changed me. Loving her had opened a place in me that not even grief had been able to shut down. The real depth, the long-lived possibilities of love, still lay within me. Gwen's love was changing me, too. Like silt in a riverbed, Gwen had stirred the shimmering promise of intimacy.

I peered into my beer glass. "There's more where that came from," I said.

A waitress paused at my table. Guiltily, I shook my head. Time to call it a night. I left a big tip. I was drunk but I wasn't a bum. I dragged myself back to my room.

In the morning, the weather had turned. Cold rain sprayed the windows, shrouding the ocean and tempting patrons to linger over coffee. I ignored the muffins and fruit and begged aspirin from the innkeeper.

"Have you been to the overlook?" she inquired. I shook my head, winced, and she gave me a map. "There's a view," she promised. I was inclined to doubt her, given the weather.

I searched for my car keys and began to zip my jacket. Before I got it all the way closed, my fingers tangled in Ryan's necklace. Briefly, I caressed the cross, then fastened my collar. I braved the sleet, ran to my car and blasted the defroster. With the harbor socked in, there was little hope of seeing anything. Sensible tourists were scurrying between the heated shops. I was the only one headed for sightseeing.

I drove up the auto road, wipers beating. Out of

the car, I hunched into my hood and approached the overlook. Clouds roiled; gray-white mist dripped like saturated wool. The white masts of the sailboats were visible, threaded through the fog like needles in linen. Below, twin peninsulas formed the cove; across the mouth, small islands splayed like a child's fingers. The ocean was gray and dull, scarcely reflective, like pewter.

I sat on a rock and watched the storm until my jeans were soaked, my joints stiff. Rivulets coursed across my shoulders, down my arms. The wind surged under my raingear, blew through my shirt and stripped my body of heat. I shivered and stayed put. The rain slackened and turned to mist, hanging like a veil between the clouds and sea. The wind made another pass, gave one more tug for the warmth in my chest, and I let it come in.

I thought of Margaret Mann, bagging Ryan's clothes for the Goodwill. I thought of Brittany, who was already strong enough to win her own medals. I thought about Julia and Mom, who would probably keep power-walking, and Dad, with his calcium and legal counsel. I thought of Gwen.

I got to my feet. I was sodden and shivering, hollow with cold. My chest ached where the wind had tunneled inside. Gradually, I became aware of a tingling sensation. My heart was beating furiously, pumping blood, circulating warmth and pushing out the chill. The tingling progressed down my arms and legs. My chest began to burn.

I loosened my collar, opened my jacket and took Ryan's cross from around my neck. It lay in my palm, beading with moisture. I raised it to my lips, kissed it and closed my hand. Then I brought my arm back and flung it, hard. The pendant flew seaward, like a slim bird. It glimmered through the veil, into the mist. Before it vanished I saw the chain, a twist of silver, like the waterfall from a long-ago hike, like the ribbons in my sister's hair.

The rain resumed, falling mercilessly until I was chilled all over again. I fumbled for my car keys, dropped them, and finally got the engine running and the heater. Back at the inn, I hung my wet clothes from the shower rack where they dripped into my hot bath. I soaked up the heat. When I was warmed through and dressed in dry clothes, I ate an early supper, sipped tea and called it a day. By dusk, I was ready for bed. I read sonnets until I fell asleep.

On Wednesday morning I left early. I could have stayed another night but I'd done enough sightseeing.

"Visit again," the innkeeper urged.

"It's a nice place," I said. But I was in a hurry to get back to Boston.

It was early afternoon when I got home. I tossed my unsorted mail onto the table and left my bag on the floor of my bedroom. My apartment felt cold. Empty. I looked around. It was clean, but the walls needed paint. My furniture, all secondhand, was old and worn. It would have to go, I decided. Time to start saving for a new bedroom set. I opened the newspaper and turned to the classifieds, scanning the rentals. Outside of Boston, I could get something more spacious. I wondered if Gwen would like a backyard. I started sorting through my belongings. I purged my dresser of old socks and yanked unworn dress shirts off hangers. I was going to have a lot more closet space. I went to the kitchen for trash bags and remembered I didn't have any food in my refrigerator. I needed packing boxes and groceries.

I stopped what I was doing and called Gwen at work.

"Andrea? Where are you?"

"My place."

"I thought you were out of town."

"I spent two days in Camden."

"Did you do anything fun?"

"Oh, bookstores, cafés. Will you come over tonight?"

"Sure."

"What do you want for dinner?"

"You decide." She hung up.

I bought garlic and onions, salad fixings and fresh tomatoes. As I was leaving the produce section, I found myself wandering into the aisle that sold greeting cards and candles. I stood still for a moment, listening. There was the usual supermarket hum — cash registers and refrigeration, but in my head, Grandma was scolding. *"You want to impress your friend, you should set a nice table."* I chose a pair of candles.

I begged some empty boxes from one of the stock clerks and headed home. I found pasta in my cupboard, and Grandma's candlesticks. She was right — the table should look nice. While the spaghetti sauce was simmering I went back to my clothes piles.

When Gwen arrived, she said, "Whatever you're cooking smells great."

"Tomato sauce."

She took a deep whiff. "I love that smell." She

surveyed my apartment. Some of the mess from the bedroom had spilled into the hall. "What's all this?"

I hadn't thought about a preamble, hadn't prepared a speech or lead-in. I faced her, hands on my hips. "I want us to live together."

"Okay."

I'd expected a fight at least, a break-up at worst.

She shrugged out of her jacket, kicked off her shoes. I wanted to watch her do that every evening. I wanted her to come into the kitchen every night and ask, "What's for dinner?"

I poured two glasses of seltzer and she took her drink to the couch.

"I'll get new furniture," I said.

"Let me do the decorating."

"Good idea." I sat beside her. "We'll get something big enough for you to have a studio. A place with good light for painting."

She said, "You need a study. Some place quiet to write."

"I want to make you happy." She laughed. "Commitment," I insisted. "I can take care of you."

"I'm not a featherweight. I'm not at the mercy of every gust of wind."

I had to agree. I'd been living my life as if at a bus stop, waiting for people — Ryan, Julia, Mom and Dad — to appear or disappear. What if I let people come and go as they pleased? Could I be so casual?

"Why now, Andrea?"

"While I was away, I said goodbye."

She looked at me with that soft expression. "I had dinner with Faye over the weekend. She's sorry you had to go through that hard time alone."

"No big deal," I mumbled.

"I told her I was serious about you and she paid for my meal."

"That sounds like Mom. The dinner part, I mean. She likes you."

"I need to come out to my parents. Faye had a few suggestions on how to break the news."

"My mother, the expert," I said.

"I had lunch with Casper yesterday."

"Oh, shit. What's going on at work?"

"I agreed to recommend him for the partnership. I get full control of creative and he'll take over as accounts director. The clients like his calm demeanor."

I absorbed the news. "You'll go for a partnership somewhere else. When do you leave?"

"I didn't spill my guts to your mother so I could say goodbye. I thought we just got past this."

"Are you really giving up the partnership?"

She was thoughtful. "It's hard to admit, but falling in love has changed my perspective."

"What's so hard to admit?" I pressed.

"That I can have you and the art. I was wrong about what I want."

I leaned closer. "What do you want, Gwen? Please tell me. Let me give it to you." My throat closed. "Let me try."

She smiled. "You inspire me. I thought you knew." While I was staring at her, she said, "Casper guessed about us. From now on, he's going to do your performance reviews."

"I can't write for him," I wailed.

"You write for me and no one else. Is that clear?"

"Yeah." I went to the kitchen and turned the heat down under the sauce. I called, "Should I start the pasta?" She didn't answer so I went back to the couch.

She had her blouse off. "Next time, let's go on vacation together."

I bent to her, unhooked her bra. "Wherever you want."

She unfastened her skirt. Her hips rose but I held her still, centered my lips between her breasts and stroked my tongue along the bone, as though it were a scalpel and I could slice her open. I closed my eyes. Her heart was round and strong, a red mass of fiber and tissue, the muscle pumping faster, then slower, filling with blood, beating and beating. I retraced the line as if to seal the incision.

It was late by the time we ate dinner, later still when Gwen fell asleep. I lay beside her, watching lights from the street play on the window, then dozing, imagining that the glow from our lovemaking was all around the bed. It was within me, too. Love was the force that tied me to life and pulled me along — twisting behind me, pouring through me, stretching endlessly ahead.

BAD MOON RISING by Barbara Johnson. 208 pp. 2nd Colleen
Fitzgerald mystery.   ISBN 1-56280-211-9 $11.95

RIVER QUAY by Janet McClellan. 208 pp. 3rd Tru North
mystery.   ISBN 1-56280-212-7   11.95

ENDLESS LOVE by Lisa Shapiro. 272 pp. To believe, once
again, that love can be forever.   ISBN 1-56280-213-5   11.95

FALLEN FROM GRACE by Pat Welch. 256 pp. 6th Helen Black
mystery.   ISBN 1-56280-209-7   11.95

THE NAKED EYE by Catherine Ennis. 208 pp. Her lover in the
camera's eye . . .   ISBN 1-56280-210-0   11.95

OVER THE LINE by Tracey Richardson. 176 pp. 2nd Stevie
Houston mystery.   ISBN 1-56280-202-X   11.95

JULIA'S SONG by Ann O'Leary. 208 pp. Strangely
disturbing . . . strangely exciting.   ISBN 1-56280-197-X   11.95

LOVE IN THE BALANCE by Marianne K. Martin. 256 pp.
Weighing the costs of love . . .   ISBN 1-56280-199-6   11.95

PIECE OF MY HEART by Julia Watts. 208 pp. All the
stuff that dreams are made of —   ISBN 1-56280-206-2   11.95

MAKING UP FOR LOST TIME by Karin Kallmaker. 240 pp.
Nobody does it better . . .   ISBN 1-56280-196-1   11.95

GOLD FEVER by Lyn Denison. 224 pp. By author of *Dream
Lover.*   ISBN 1-56280-201-1   11.95

WHEN THE DEAD SPEAK by Therese Szymanski. 224 pp. 2nd
Brett Higgins mystery.   ISBN 1-56280-198-8   11.95

FOURTH DOWN by Kate Calloway. 240 pp. 4th Cassidy James
mystery.   ISBN 1-56280-205-4   11.95

A MOMENT'S INDISCRETION by Peggy J. Herring. 176 pp.
There's a fine line between love and lust . . . ISBN 1-56280-194-5   11.95

CITY LIGHTS/COUNTRY CANDLES by Penny Hayes. 208 pp.
About the women she has known . . .   ISBN 1-56280-195-3   11.95

POSSESSIONS by Kaye Davis. 240 pp. 2nd Maris Middleton
mystery.   ISBN 1-56280-192-9   11.95

A QUESTION OF LOVE by Saxon Bennett. 208 pp. Every
woman is granted one great love.   ISBN 1-56280-205-4   11.95

RHYTHM TIDE by Frankie J. Jones. 160 pp.   . . . to desire
passionately and be passionately desired.   ISBN 1-56280-189-9   11.95

PENN VALLEY PHOENIX by Janet McClellan. 208 pp. 2nd
Tru North Mystery.   ISBN 1-56280-200-3   11.95

BY RESERVATION ONLY by Jackie Calhoun. 240 pp. A
chance for true happiness.   ISBN 1-56280-191-0   11.95

OLD BLACK MAGIC by Jaye Maiman. 272 pp. 9th Robin
Miller mystery.   ISBN 1-56280-175-9   11.95

LEGACY OF LOVE by Marianne K. Martin. 240 pp. Women
will do anything for her . . .   ISBN 1-56280-184-8   11.95

LETTING GO by Ann O'Leary. 160 pp. Laura, at 39, in love
with 23-year-old Kate.   ISBN 1-56280-183-X   11.95

LADY BE GOOD edited by Barbara Grier and Christine Cassidy.
288 pp. Erotic stories by Naiad Press authors.   ISBN 1-56280-180-5   14.95

CHAIN LETTER by Claire McNab. 288 pp. 9th Carol Ashton
mystery.   ISBN 1-56280-181-3   11.95

NIGHT VISION by Laura Adams. 256 pp. Erotic fantasy romance
by "famous" author.   ISBN 1-56280-182-1   11.95

SEA TO SHINING SEA by Lisa Shapiro. 256 pp. Unable to resist
the raging passion . . .   ISBN 1-56280-177-5   11.95

THIRD DEGREE by Kate Calloway. 224 pp. 3rd Cassidy James
mystery.   ISBN 1-56280-185-6   11.95

WHEN THE DANCING STOPS by Therese Szymanski. 272 pp.
1st Brett Higgins mystery.   ISBN 1-56280-186-4   11.95

PHASES OF THE MOON by Julia Watts. 192 pp. . . . . . hungry
for everything life has to offer.   ISBN 1-56280-176-7   11.95

BABY IT'S COLD by Jaye Maiman. 256 pp. 5th Robin Miller
mystery.   ISBN 1-56280-156-2   10.95

These are just a few of the many Naiad Press titles — we are the oldest and
largest lesbian/feminist publishing company in the world. We also offer an
enormous selection of lesbian video products. Please request a complete
catalog. We offer personal service; we encourage and welcome direct mail
orders from individuals who have limited access to bookstores carrying our
publications.